"A series of brilliantly told adventures . . . Frontier Alaska is described with vivid and loving detail. Haldeman is a magnificent writer and the details and characters are superb. Reaching a place where the science fiction experience passes close to mysticism, *Guardian* doesn't try to fit into any of the conventional science fiction pigeonholes."
—*The Denver Post*

"An amazingly fine historical novel . . . Haldeman is a marvelous storyteller."
—*Rocky Mountain News*

"Joe Haldeman is an excellent writer . . . He does wonderful work."
—*The San Diego Union-Tribune*

"Haldeman is a skilled stylist. He writes thoughtful books, rich with characterization. But who knew he could so completely get into the head of a woman born in 1858? That this master of science fiction, who has made the interior of spaceships and the far reaches of space so believable, could also so readily bring to life the world of the Midwest and Alaska in the latter part of the nineteenth century? Trust me, he does. Haldeman conveys the voice of the character perfectly, so much so that you never really think about who's actually writing the book: a male professor at MIT and Vietnam vet. He also does a wonderful job describing this lost time, from train travel and railroad strikes to steamboats and life in the rough mining towns that provided the launching basis for prospectors on their way to the gold fields. Highly recommended."
—Charles de Lint

"Haldeman craft[s] a solid tale . . . [He] must be commended for his meticulous re-creation of period America. As a richly sensual evocation of the late-nineteenth century United States, this book will surely captivate the reader looking for exotic wonders of the recent past. From the technology of steam travel to the odd cuisine to the cultural attitudes of the average citizen, Haldeman re-creates a vanished era and plunks the reader firmly into it. Furthermore, the first-person narration by Rosa is flawlessly done. We fully believe in the three-dimensionality of this woman, and inhabit her sensibility fully. Bruce Sterling recently propounded the question: Could honest and vital SF with real speculative impact be set in the historical past without cheating either history or SF? Almost as if in answer, Haldeman's novel proves that SF is up to such challenges."

—*Off the Shelf*

"A compelling and economical narrative . . . Rosa Coleman is one of Haldeman's characteristically indomitable and competent women characters, and in some ways she may be the most humanly convincing of all of them . . . Haldeman manages Rosa's narrative voice with a brilliantly controlled sense of tone, and the tale of her cross-continent odyssey is strong enough to sustain the novel even without its late blossoming of SF conceits . . . *Guardian* is a compelling tale, demonstrating that Haldeman's vaunted skill at the integration of character and setting is equally at home in the past as in the future."

—Gary K. Wolfe, *Locus*

"Elegantly written, with fully developed characters and a well-researched historical setting."

—*SF Site*

"An evocation of America in the last quarter of the nineteenth century, its big cities and Midwestern farm towns, its trains and riverboats and ferries and tramp steamers. But the big set-piece is a reconstruction of the staggering grounds for the Alaskan gold rush, a story-within-a-story that is built with loving attention and must be one of the book's reasons for being . . . Whether the setting is cosmic or quotidian, Joe Haldeman is so good at what he does that it doesn't matter which genre he chooses to stay within or sprawl beyond."

—Russell Letson, *Locus*

"The descriptions of the nineteenth-century West are highly evocative and the characters are well-drawn. Haldeman's vivid and descriptive passages evoke a feeling for what life must have really been like for people seeking their fortunes in the gold fields of the Yukon."

—*SFRevu.com*

GUARDIAN

Joe Haldeman

ACE BOOKS, NEW YORK

This is a work of fiction. Names, characters, places, and incidents either are the product of the author's imagination or are used fictitiously, and any resemblance to actual persons, living or dead, business establishments, events, or locales is entirely coincidental.

GUARDIAN

An Ace Book / published by arrangement with the author

PRINTING HISTORY
Ace hardcover edition / December 2002
Ace mass market edition / August 2004

Copyright © 2002 by Joe Haldeman.
Cover art by Craig White.
Cover design by Rita Frangie.

ISBN: 0-441-01106-3

ACE®
Ace Books are published by The Berkley Publishing Group,
a division of Penguin Group (USA) Inc.,
375 Hudson Street, New York, New York 10014.
ACE and The "A" design
are trademarks belonging to Penguin Group (USA) Inc.

PRINTED IN THE UNITED STATES OF AMERICA

10 9 8 7 6 5 4 3 2 1

This book is dedicated to my brother Jay, who (as Jack C. Haldeman II) wrote eight science fiction novels and over a hundred short stories—and also dedicated to Alaska, where we had the good fortune to live as children.

The state is calling itself "our last, best hope" now, which may or may not be true. It is probably the best place to raise a child if for some reason you want him or her to become a science fiction writer. The beauty and size of it, the limitless possibilities. The amazing sky.

I also want to thank the Clutes, John and Judith. John, for clueing me in on the Flammarion novel that eerily parallels this one; Judith, for leading me on a wild bicycle ride through the labyrinthine streets of London, to their huge book collection, where we actually found an English translation of it.

One character's name was changed to memorialize Gordon R. Dickson, who took many of us to places we wouldn't have found on our own.

GUARDIAN

When my father died in 2004, aged 105, he left behind this manuscript, with a letter saying that I could publish it if I wished to.

I don't see why not, though I will call it a work of fiction, or of wishing, rather than a memoir. Much of it is impossible to believe, though it is presented as fact. I am of an age myself, 77 this month, able to appreciate the fact that the membrane that separates memory from imagination is semipermeable at best.

It's the story of Rosa Coleman, my father's mother,

whom I knew as G-ma at the end of her long life. She was born before the Civil War.

G-ma told me many stories when I was a boy, but never this one. Her son, my famous father, never mentioned it either, understandably. His great fear was ending his days in an institution, and that is probably where he would have wound up if he had presented this as truth.

But Pops thought enough of it to go to some trouble and expense to have it typed up and carefully preserved.

She was a sweet woman, the joy of my childhood, and I offer her story here with respect and no further comment.

—Blake Coleman
21 March 2005

DECEMBER 29TH, 1952

I have started to write this down many times in the past twenty years—ever since I turned seventy, and felt that every day of life was a special gift. Like many an old woman, I've chosen to spend that gift on my grandchildren and their children, with the odd moment or hour given over to the church, and do not regret any of that.

But last month I had a small stroke and though I

have recovered most of my faculties, it's obvious that I have outstayed my welcome on this world. I do have a strange story to tell, and have put off telling it for too long.

Parts of the story would be embarrassing to my son, especially in his particular prominence—so I have agreed to leave this book in his keeping, not to be printed until after his death, or even after the death of his own son.

Perhaps from that distant perspective, the more fantastic parts of this account will seem less strange.

During the Depression, I helped support my family by writing stories for the pulp magazines, under a variety of male pseudonyms. I stopped writing during the War, paper shortages having closed most of my markets, and never went back to it. But I was skillful with dialogue in those days, and with the reader's indulgence I will have recourse to that artifice in this memoir. Of course I don't remember the exact words of conversations more than a half-century old. I do remember having had the conversations, though, and trust that I can reconstruct the sense of them.

My son has set me up in this unused parlor with a comfortable desk and chair and a bookshelf with all of my diaries. I count forty-three of them, most of them covering more than one year. The earliest starts in 1868, when I was ten, but nothing of much interest happens in my life until the nineties.

Still, a few things for the record, as they say nowadays. I was born in Helen's Mill, Georgia, in 1858, on a plantation with slaves. I remember almost nothing of that except the image of a large Negro woman, who I'm told was my nurse Daisy. I'm told I played with the slave children.

All of the children (the white children) in the family were sent to stay with relatives in Philadelphia after Fort Sumter, in 1861. My father correctly divined that the war would not go that far north. Though Gettysburg was close enough that we knew people who went out to watch the battle, and hear the speeches afterwards.

Sherman's troops burned our plantation just before Atlanta, and I suppose my mother and father died during that invasion. We never heard from them again.

There was really no room for myself and my sisters and brother with Aunt Karen and Uncle Claude, so I was sent to Dorothy Partridge's Boarding School, a strict Methodist place where I stayed until rescued by Wellesley in 1875.

Some of the girls complained about Wellesley's strictness, but to me it was emancipation. At Partridge's we had supervised prayer five times a day. Miss Partridge could read your mind, and she saw nothing there but sin. When we were actually caught in sin, we were sent to the Forgiveness Room, a dark closet with nothing but a large candle, a prayer rail, and a chamber pot with no cover. A truly bad sin, like sneaking in candy, would put you in that room for twenty-four hours, with no food or water and little air, sore from the switch or the rod. So to me the proctors and housemistresses of Wellesley were nothing. At worst, they might send me to a detention room, with only a Bible to contemplate. But that was no punishment at all. I've always enjoyed reading the Bible, trying to puzzle things out.

At this end of my life, there is much to puzzle over for which the Bible is little help. But I still read it daily, peering now through a magnifying glass. Even this large-type version is too difficult for my spectacles alone.

At Wellesley I studied natural philosophy and literature. I suppose it was as good a preparation as a woman could have, then or now, for the strange trials I was to face with the Raven.

I shouldn't call them trials, because they were not intended as such. My actual trials, most of a century's physical and mental pain, have been provided by myself and other humans, and they have not been as great as most people's.

The odd journey begins.

Wellesley was a gift from my parents and their slaves. Like many people in the South, they foresaw the end of our "peculiar institution" long before the Emancipation Proclamation. There was no shortage of investors willing to gamble that they were wrong, though, and so they sold all of the slaves, and leased the plantation as well. Father sold all of them as a group, though they would have brought much more at auction. He didn't want to break up families, and he was disgusted to learn that the babies would not only be separated from their mothers, but be sold by the pound, like so much beef.

My older brother Roland claimed that at least one of the Negro babies was Father's own. He was twelve when we came north, so perhaps he was old enough to know. But he also bore a grudge against Father, because each of us girl children got a larger stipend than his.

We were lucky to have anything. If Father had delayed the sale another year, he would have been paid in Confederate currency, ultimately worthless. As it was, he was paid partly in gold, and hired an agent to bear a small chest of double eagles to a Philadelphia bank, and there open trust accounts for each of us. We knew nothing of this until Ronald turned eighteen in 1866, and was granted access to his account, several hundred dollars, which he spent soon enough, living in a grand style.

By then we were dismally sure that our parents were dead. We had last heard from them in 1864, a hasty note my mother sent to Aunt Karen. They were abandoning the general store in Helen's Mill (which they had bought after leaving the plantation), because Sherman's monsters were only a day away. They moved into Atlanta for protection.

The Philadelphia paper with Mathew Brady's photographs of the ruins of Atlanta was kept from me, as I was only eight. Of course, I found them soon enough on my own. This century's images of Hiroshima and Dresden have a similar impact now. But I knew no one in those places. The sepia landscapes of Atlanta's ashes are the only memorial of my parents' time and place of death.

I've visited many places in this world, and elsewhere, but I've never been to Atlanta. I did drive down to Georgia in the 1920s, to find what was left of Helen's Mill—not even memories—but managed to do it on dirt roads that didn't go through that horrible city.

By the time I was seventeen, I believe Dorothy Partridge was as tired of me as I was of her. I was told that there was a sum available adequate to see me through college, and I took the examinations for Mount Holyoke and Wellesley.

I passed both, but wound up choosing Wellesley, for various reasons. Both Boston and Harvard were nearby, and Philadelphia was agreeably distant. It was a new school then, beginning its fifth year.

Perhaps it was not the best choice for me; perhaps I would not have been an outstanding scholar anywhere. I made no lasting friendships there, and was an indifferent student and terrible athlete. We were encouraged to engage in physical activities like gymnastics and the newly fashionable lawn tennis, which at the time seemed mannish and unnatural to me. (Could I have foreseen my coarse life to come, in Kansas and Alaska, I wouldn't have believed it.)

At the time there were critics of female higher education who claimed that athletics would overexcite us and lead us into unwholesome practices. I found it boring and tiring—and, I have to admit, more than half believed that overexertion would lead me into some mysterious nameless state of sin, which terrified me. I knew almost nothing about sex, except that it was all about sin and shame and pain.

If at any time in my life I needed a friend, it was then. I was surrounded by girls and young women who were sophisticated and cosmopolitan, who might have brought me fast into real life. But my background cut me off from them—I was a slow-witted Southern belle with no social graces and no family connections—and once ostracized, I tried to make a virtue out of my separateness.

I was also beautiful in those days, at least to people other than myself, which didn't help. To the boys I was an exotic Southern flower, and I can see now that my terror of them, and subsequent awkward rejection, made me a valuable prize, and further cut me off from the other women—who of course saw my clumsiness as shameless and artful seduction.

So my fondest memories of college are all times of solitude. Reading in the library or long walks in the woods and fields. When the weather was fine I would paint or draw, but I enjoyed the walks even when it was storming or I had to pick my way through the snow. Most Saturdays I would walk unescorted around Boston and Cambridge, which produced a little tingle of danger.

My original plan had been to study theology, both out of a natural inclination and a sense that I might eventually do some good with it. But my inability with languages, which had earned me beatings and confinement at the hands of Mrs. Partridge, kept me from that course of study. I had no Latin and less Greek, as someone said. Most of my classmates had studied both for years. I had just managed to drag my way through French.

As if in compensation, I discovered an ability with mathematics, losing myself for hours at a time in trigonometry, geometry plane and not so plain, algebra, and calculus. I also had enthusiasm for natural philosophy and natural history, both terms subsumed under "science" long since.

I studied as much biology and astronomy as was

offered at the nonspecialist level, and then pursued astronomy as far as my mathematics would allow. It was a congenial study for me, solitary under the night sky at the school's small observatory, making careful measurements, and doing pencil and ink drawings of the moon and planets. I didn't feel I had the intellect or drive to become a professional astronomer—there were only two or three women so employed in the whole country—but I did aspire to teach.

(Professor Sarah Whiting was my mentor there, an intense, energetic woman who wanted more for me than I wanted for myself. The year I graduated, she found her true protégée in Annie Jump Cannon, who wound up, at Harvard, becoming the first famous woman astronomer in America. I met Annie some years later, and she confided that her whole career pivoted on a fluke of fate: she was getting through Harvard working as a maid, when an exasperated astronomer yelled at his assistant, "My *maid* could do a better job than that!" She could indeed, and she got the job.)

Insofar as I could divine my future, I saw a period of teaching in a school for girls somewhere in New England, eventually to meet a man whom I could tolerate or even love, and settle into the roles of wife and mother. At Wellesley I fell into church work, teaching Bible class to children aged six through nine, and I adored it, and assumed that would continue as well. Of course the only reliable thing that one can say about one's future is that it will not turn out the way you planned it. People who have no interest in your future pass through your life and change it forever.

In my case it was nothing so direct and dramatic as Annie Jump Cannon's exasperated astronomer. I was asked—ordered—to go to dinner and the opera.

Meeting the monster.

It happened to be St. Valentine's Day, and most of the women in my dormitory were getting ready for a ball at Harvard. The housemistress came knocking on doors, totally flustered, asking whether anyone was free—her brother was in Boston on business, and he needed a companion. He'd accepted an invitation to dinner and the opera with two associates and their wives, and didn't want to be a fifth wheel, odd man out; whatever it was we said in those days. I was the only one who had no plans for the evening, so there was no room for discussion: I was "it."

I didn't much like the housemistress, a prissy stern woman; nor was I in any mood to be sociable, cross with my flux just starting—but I agreed sweetly, privately promising myself that I would give her brother an engagement he would not soon forget.

The evening began impressively. When I came down I found not the usual hired cab, but a well-appointed Brewster coach, complete with footman. (That would be like a liveried driver in a Cadillac today.) It was even warm inside, with a brazier.

It was a swift and comfortable ride into the city, but I held on to my resolve to make this Mr. Tolliver pay dearly for taking me away from my studies. Warned by the ostentatious coach that he would be wealthy and not modest, I was not surprised when we pulled up at the Parker House.

A servant led me to a lounge where the great man was waiting with his guests. I was not immediately impressed. Edward Tolliver was a tall, powerful-looking man, coarse-featured and loud. He was cordial but stiff with me and the other women; hearty with the men.

At dinner I was only as ladylike as I had to be, offering opinions more freely than I normally would do, but he actually seemed to like that, and was amused by my unladylike appetite. I was starving, hours past my normal suppertime, and had a large Porterhouse steak and plenty of claret with it—actually one of the most enjoyable meals I'd ever been served. And one of the best I would ever have, as a human.

He was nine years older than me, too young to have fought in the war. He had a law degree from Harvard but practiced in Philadelphia, so we did have that in common, as well as Southern origins, which surprised both of us. Neither of us retained much of the South in our speech, at least around Northerners; he sounded as Bostonian as any of the others.

I was afraid that the heavy meal and wine might put me to sleep at the theater, especially if we rode there in the warm coach, so I asked whether we might walk, and meet the others there. He readily agreed; it was only a few blocks down Tremont. The night was brisk and he was much more at ease, witty and almost charming, away from the others.

I should not have worried about sleeping through the opera, which was *Carmen,* new that year to these shores and most exciting. Afterwards, we went back to the Parker House and had coffee and cakes, and I returned to Wellesley scandalously late, after one in the morning.

Edward wrote me weekly from Philadelphia, letters that were friendly rather than romantic, but soon it was obvious what his intentions were. I was afraid that the woman he was attracted to was not actually me, but rather the consciously forward "modern" girl I had masqueraded as, and eventually I got up the courage to write him to that effect. He responded by returning to Boston, ostensibly to meet whoever the actual "me" was.

This was the Easter break of my senior year. We saw each other daily for more than a week. Savory lunches at the Parker House and other ostentatious places.

In the evenings we had to be chaperoned by his sister, my housemistress, which was annoying. I felt capable of protecting my own virtue, and besides had had more than enough of her company.

I might have been grateful for her interference, had I known him as well as I came to. On the other hand, if he had shown his true colors during that courtship, I never would have married him.

Sometimes I consider that: what if I had married a nice man instead, and settled down to a regular life in Boston or Philadelphia, or wherever. The worlds I would have missed. This world would have been far different, too.

If Gordon had never been born, this world could be a lifeless radioactive ball.

But I didn't have a *crystal* ball. I was swept away by his attentions and charmed by his clumsy gallantry—he was much more attractive to me than a more polished, polite man would have been, with his obvious struggle to do and say the right things, keeping in check an elemental force that intrigued me.

I was too naive to see that force for what it was: raw sexual desire, and the need to dominate.

It was an unusually clement spring—I remember a blizzard on Easter morning, another year—and we ranged all around the area in a nimble calash that he hired and drove himself. Downtown Boston was a noisome cesspool in the thaw, as always, so most of our travels were out in the country, going as far as Salem on occasion. We picnicked and chatted; I learned a lot about the masculine worlds of finance and law, and he paid polite attention to my ramblings about nature and art and literature.

After ten days, he proposed to me, with a diamond ring that I supposed was worth more than I owned. He wanted me to come back to Philadelphia with him, right then!—and was not amused when *I* was amused, saying that I was not about to go to college for three and a half years, only to leave with no degree. He argued with some force that I would never need the degree; I would never need to work. He had come into a fortune at twenty-one, and it had grown constantly since.

What is clear now is that he wanted to cut short my education so as to limit my potential for independence. If I could work, I could leave him, though of course in 1879 that would never have entered my mind. Divorce was an exotic thing that degenerate foreigners did, or free-thinking atheists.

He did grudgingly wait. We were married right after my graduation, in the largest Episcopalian church in Philadelphia. There were hundreds in attendance, though not a dozen on my side of the aisle. Most of them were "codfish aristocracy," people who had actually made money rather than being born into it. (Edward was not Episcopalian, or anything else. The church was chosen for status and size.)

There were so many flowers that I nearly choked on their cloying ambience. I managed not to sneeze until we were outside the church.

In retrospect I suppose it was vulgar and dishonest, if honesty mandated mutual love and respect before holy matrimony. I did love Edward in a naive, schoolgirl way, and Edward had reached an age and station where not having a wife and family was considered peculiar. He set out to find an upper-class woman who was both beautiful and educated. That my "aristocratic" family was a thousand miles away and destitute was a real advantage to a man who wanted absolute control over his life, and especially over his wife.

His unspeakable brutality.

Our bridal trip was to the New Jersey shore, which could be beautiful when the wind and tide cooperated. Otherwise, the detritus of New York City befouled the beaches. It was too cool for bathing, which I remember as a major physical disappointment—my nuptial duties, fulfilled frequently and with no patience, left me in a state that Edward laughingly called "saddle-sore."

I was immediately with child, but lost the little one, my only girl, in four months' time. My third and fourth pregnancies also ended in miscarriages. It would be fifty years before medical science identified the Rh factor, but evidently that was our problem. Edward blamed it on some female weakness, and I was poked at and peered inside by specialists in New York and Boston as well as Philadelphia.

My second baby was small, two months prematature, but he survived. Daniel was a charming infant, naturally well-tempered, easily amused and amusing. After a slow start, he grew fast, and by two was big and strong for his age.

When it became clear that he had a son and heir, Edward stopped having sexual relations with me, at least of a kind that could result in pregnancy. What he did was painful and degrading, and I would think a sin, for its unnaturalness. But he said it was for my own sake, and there was nothing in the Bible about it, unless it were men done with men.

He only came to me about once a month. He "worked late" often, though, and gossips told me he was often seen down by Drury Lane at night, an area full of prostitutes. In 1890 I found out that he had been supporting a mistress for years, keeping her on the firm's books as an apprentice.

When I confronted him with this, he beat me so soundly that I lost a tooth. I should have left him then. He apologized, weeping, for his "nature," and bought me a ruby necklace. We made up an excuse about a carriage accident, and a dentist crafted me a replacement tooth of porcelain.

I looked back through my diaries and found that he had beaten me fifteen times in ten years, badly enough for me to record it. I went so far as to talk to my minister about it, although of course I left out the sexual details.

He was a kindly man, and offered to talk to Edward, but I thought that would certainly make things worse. He quoted scripture to me, which I already knew, about a woman's place and obligations.

It was clear in my mind that the church and its ministers were fallible, and I still might have left him if it were just me. But Daniel loved him madly as a child, in spite of similar beatings, which at the time we thought were natural between father and son. Edward spent a lot of time with him when he was growing up, teaching him how to fish and sail and ride, and practicing sports with him. They laid out a small baseball diamond in the backyard, and installed a canvas pad in the basement, for boxing and wrestling.

One Sunday in 1894, the servants out of the house, I heard a strange sound from the basement, a strained whimpering, and I opened the door slightly and peeked down. There on the boxing mat, my husband had pulled down their garments and was having his son the way he had me, like two dogs coupling. He had his hand over Daniels' mouth, but couldn't quite muzzle his agonized grunts.

I ran upstairs to where Edward kept his pistols, but there was no ammunition in sight, and I wasn't really sure how to load and fire one. So I went to the kitchen and got a large cleaver.

When I returned to the basement door, they were finished. Edward was buttoning up his clothing and spoke in harsh whispers to our son, cowering half naked on the mat.

Daniel saw me looking down, and at his expression I eased the door shut. I would find some more sure and safe way to deal with this.

I was in the kitchen making tea cookies when Edward came up. He said that Daniel had been slightly injured in their wrestling practice, and I was not to be worried if he had tears. After all, he was only fourteen.

There was a large knife on the counter, and only God's hand stayed me, saved me, from plunging it into his heart.

He went upstairs to change, and then left for the

club, his Sunday round of golf and cards. I waited for Daniel to come up, but he didn't, and after some time I finally went down to the basement.

He was sitting in the darkest corner, quiet, not crying. He asked whether he might launder his clothing alone. I said that he could, but I knew more about such things. I haltingly told him his father had used me the same way, and we cried together.

I washed the blood from his unmentionables and mixed an astringent poultice for him to apply. I told him to take a bath and then pack everything he could not live without into a small trunk. We were leaving.

I was so agitated my heart was leaping in my chest. Trying to sort out my thoughts—how to get away, where to go—I went out on the back porch, for some fresh air. I closed my eyes and tried to think clearly. Then opened them at the sound of clashing wings.

There on the wooden steps was a black bird larger than any crow I had ever seen, a raven. He hopped up two steps and cocked his head at me. "No. Gold," he said.

I knew they could be trained to talk. But why would he be taught those two words?

He hopped closer. "No!" He squawked. "Gold!" In an explosion of feathers he flew past me, out into the backyard. He perched on the birdbath and repeated, "No gold!" Then he flew away.

I was completely unnerved by the experience. But then I wondered whether it might have been a sign. And the truth was immediately clear.

I ran up to the bath and spoke to Daniel through the door. "Don't rush, darling. We can't leave until tomorrow morning."

"But Father won't be home until late," he said in a voice strained with fear. "We can run all day."

I told him no, I had thought it through, and that would be disastrous. We would be almost penniless unless I could get to the bank Monday morning, for my gold. And I had seven ladies coming for afternoon tea; if I weren't here, they would suspect the worst, and there would be police looking for us high and low.

I heard him splashing and he came out dripping wet, a towel around his waist. "What gold?"

"It's left over from my father's bequest, over a hundred twenty-dollar gold pieces. I've never told your father about it." I didn't tell him about the bird's warning. There was enough sudden strangeness in his world.

He nodded with a strangely adult, calculating look. "We could go anyplace with two thousand dollars."

"We'll leave right after he goes to the office tomorrow," I said. "Take the first train to New York City. Then on to someplace where nobody will know us."

"Can I choose?" he asked, and I said of course, but think it over. It would have to be someplace that didn't cost a fortune to get to, where I could get a job, where we wouldn't stand out. Not the Belgian Congo or Antarctica. That made him gay. I told him which trunk to fill, and he went off to sort through his things.

I had to wait by the cookies; the woodstove was unpredictable, and I had to go by the smell of the baking. I started packing in my head, though. Books: only ones that couldn't be replaced by mail order, because of long attachment. In poetry, Palgrave's *Golden Treasury* and Shakespeare's *Sonnets*. The *Treasure Island* and *Huckleberry Finn* I had read to Daniel. Perhaps I might have another child someday.

I would need sturdy, plain clothes and one of my two velvet dresses, for church and interviews; a chemise for sleeping. A dark Gibson Girl outfit for classroom or office, wherever I'd be working, perhaps two of them. I thought with longing of the huge Saratoga, that held all the clothes I could need for weeks in Boston or New York. But I wanted no more than a porter could easily carry; small enough for me to handle alone, if need be.

My drawing equipment and watercolors, leaving behind the oils and their so-called portable easel. My diaries and two or three sketchbooks, the most recent. I hated to leave the others behind; it literally was leaving a part of my self behind. But they were too bulky.

I would fill new ones. The prospect of having a new world to draw and paint gave me a sudden lift in spirits.

If I had known how literally true that would be!

Daniel came down carrying the atlas. He opened it to Kansas and pointed to Dodge City.

Well, why not? It was the ends of the earth, but that was what I wanted. If I couldn't get a job there—teaching or rounding up cattle, or whatever single women did there who didn't want to be "soiled doves"—we could move to Kansas City or St. Louis.

I warned him not to be too disappointed if there weren't a lot of gunfights and cowboys. He said sure; he knew that was all dime novel stuff, but his eyes glittered with excitement. I hoped he wouldn't be too let down by the reality.

He filled the large teakettle with water and hoisted it up on the stove while I took out the cookies and arranged them on plates to cool. Ginger, vanilla, and chocolate smells, mingling for the last time. I wrapped a few warm ones for Daniel, and sent him out to the library while I entertained the church ladies.

He asked whether he could check out books, or would that be stealing?—trying to pull an innocent face that made us both laugh. I told him I wasn't ready to begin a life of crime.

As I watched him scamper out, though, I realized that it might be just that. Taking the son of a wealthy Philadelphia lawyer might be kidnapping, even if you were the son's mother. But I put that out of my mind. Edward would never have us pursued, knowing what we could tell the authorities.

He had political ambitions. The charge of incestual sodomy might cost him some votes.

In retrospect I see how dangerously I underestimated his capacity for what I then would have called evil—for what his black anger might drive him to, finding that I had stolen the one possession he could never replace. Dodge City might have been the ends of the earth, but it wouldn't be far enough.

Putting the tea things together, I had to wonder how much of this I would be giving up. I wouldn't miss the society of the proper, stuffy church ladies. But I always looked forward to the two who were chatty and fun, Eleanor and Roxanne. Would there be enough women, proper women, in Dodge City to put together tea parties like this? Would there even be tea?

I could afford to take a tin of my favorite, the Fortnum & Mason from London. I looked longingly at the two tea services, but no. No room for indulgence. I would get us a sturdy teapot and two cups in the New York station, waiting for the train west.

The tea party was excruciatingly long and slow. I had to feign interest in church politics and minor scandal while my mind was spinning with the horror of what I'd seen in the basement and the giddy hope of escape.

Daniel came in when the last of them left; he'd been waiting in the park across the street. At the library he'd found a book on Kansas and had written out three pages from it. I read it while he had some cool sweet tea and cleaned up the cookie fragments.

Then we went upstairs and each packed and repacked our small trunks. They were awkward to handle, but Daniel improvised a lashing from two strips of leather he'd found down in the stable, so we could lift them together, each of us taking one side. I allowed him to bring his precious guitar. In fact, he looked jaunty and handsome in his traveling clothes, guitar slung around his back.

I wished we could just walk out the door and leave. But the key to our freedom resided in a safe-deposit box I couldn't open on Sunday.

So I assembled a pot roast to cook slowly and straightened up the parlor and kitchen, which usually I would have left for the maid, even though Edward might grumble about the mess. I wanted to treat him with the utmost solicitude, so he would leave in the morning content and unsuspecting.

He came home late, flushed with drink and dangerously quiet. I had already given Daniel his supper and sent him to bed, to get a good night's sleep for "school" tomorrow. Edward toyed with his food and drank most of a bottle of wine, and then wordlessly tramped upstairs, and into Daniel's room.

Afraid of what he might do with the boy, I followed silently a minute later and listened at the door. They were only talking quietly. I hid in the laundry closet across the hall, ready to use a flatiron on him if need be. But he emerged twenty minutes later and went down to the parlor. I heard glass clinking and smelled his cigar, so I cracked Daniel's door a bit and asked if he were well. He said he was all right and I bade him good night; good morrow. He repeated "good morrow" so brightly I knew he wouldn't sleep much.

If he had told me then what he was to tell me on the train the next day, I might have gone downstairs and cracked Edward's precious brandy decanter across his skull. He had made the child pray for forgiveness, for having tempted his father into sin, and promise that he would put away all sinful thoughts and not mention this to anyone, or burn in hell.

The boy did take that for what it was worth, nothing, but it renewed my fury at Edward. That abuse of a father's authority could only undermine an impressionable child's trust in God's authority as well. In later years I was to fight a hard battle, not wholly won, against Daniel's constant doubting and attraction to atheism, and I hope his father's soul is heavily burdened with his responsibility for that, on top of everything else.

We make our escape.

When the servants arrived in the morning, I treated it like any other day, though I knew that might make our later departure suspicious. Let them suspect; by evening, it would be clear enough what had happened.

How much more difficult and chancy our escape would have been today, with universal telephones and modern record-keeping. It would be impossible not to leave traces everywhere.

As it was, we had a substantial breakfast together—enjoying Sue Anne's delicious apple pancakes for the last time!—and I went through the ritual of getting

Daniel ready for school. Edward took him aside for a few words before he left for the office. As soon as his carriage was around the corner, I sent Jimmy, the stable boy, to go down to the stand on Market and send us a cabriolet.

He came back riding on its fender and, helped by the scullery maid, put our two chests aboard. We said we were taking some things out to Edward's sister in Bristol, about thirty miles away, and would be back by nightfall. I'm sure that Sue Anne, at least, suspected something was odd by my tone of voice, and Jimmy looked quizzically at the guitar, but said nothing. Daniel was trying to act nonchalant, but he trembled somewhat and looked queer. I knew he was on the verge of tears. However much he wanted to escape Edward, he was still leaving the only home he'd ever known. Jimmy had been his playmate and protector since he was small, and Sue Anne his nurse.

We got aboard the cab, and I directed the driver to the local rail line. After a couple of blocks, when we could no longer be seen from the house, I said to take us instead to the Fidelity Safe Deposit Company and wait there for me.

This safe-deposit box was the one big secret I had always withheld from Edward. It held the balance of the double eagles left over from my father's legacy, after my education. There was still enough to add a couple of pounds to my purse. I changed twelve of them into paper money and returned to the cab, which then took us to Broad Street Station.

I gave two urchins pennies to carry our chests, which was less conspicuous then carrying them ourselves, and found that our timing was nearly perfect. There was a train leaving for Jersey City Station in New York in ten minutes. We secured first-class seats and the train chugged out just as we were getting settled.

We had two facing seats to ourselves, so we spread out all the timetables I had secured at the ticket counter, and considered the various routes to Dodge City.

Privately I assumed the worst: What could Edward do if he correctly divined our course of action? It would not take him long to realize we had taken the train, and he would assume we had gone to either New York or Washington. (There was a direct train to Chicago, the Pennsylvania Limited, but it didn't leave until much later.) He could wire both places and have agents look for us. But he wouldn't be home from work until five thirty at the earliest—more like seven, most nights—and if the train was on time, we would be in New York by quarter past three.

There were dozens of trains bound from New York

to Chicago. It was just possible he could have an agent watching for us there. In fact, we would probably be well advised not to go through Chicago at all, since if he guessed we were westward bound, he would have that station watched.

I told Daniel we might as well see a lot of the country, and charted a jagged path that put us on the four o'clock to Pittsburgh, and from there one of the trains to Buffalo. Down to Cleveland the next morning, then back up to Gary, Indiana, and over to Davenport, Iowa, where we would pick up the Rock Island Line and get off at Kansas City. From there, we could take a stagecoach to Dodge, if there was no local passenger line. (I knew that Dodge owed its existence to a freight line, laid down originally for the buffalo hunters, and then used for cattle.)

Daniel drew a careful map, with times. I talked about how fun it would be to see Niagara Falls and the Mississippi, which confused him for a moment. "But aren't we just trying to keep Father from catching us?" I told him we could do two things at once, and resolved to be as frank with him as possible.

That frankness never extended to the incident that had precipitated our flight. We never referred to it directly for many years. In fact, my only diary reference about it, my final diary entry of many thousand in

Philadelphia, was *Edward has done the unspeakable. We leave tomorrow, come what may. God protect us.*

Jersey City Station was crowded and noisy but agreeably free of smoke and cinders. They "coasted" the trains in, without power, which was quiet and eerie until the shriek of brakes.

I booked us on the four o'clock, declining to have our luggage checked through, in case we had to change plans quickly. Then I sat with our things and sent Daniel off with a dollar to buy some fruit and something to read. He came back with two apples and a number of magazines of a type Edward did not allow in the house—story papers like *Saturday Night* and *The Argosy.* (I used to get that one almost every week when Daniel was younger, back when it was *The Golden Argosy.* But now it was hardly a magazine for children.) He also had a couple of dime novels that I supposed qualified as "research" for our ultimate destination.

(I had recently read about Dodge City and knew that it was no longer so wild and wooly as it had been in the seventies—"the Beautiful Bibulous Babylon of the Frontier"—because the cattle drives that had provided the town with all those rowdy cowboys were long a thing of the past. I was less worried about gunfights than about finding a job.)

I had picked a corner to wait in where I would be inconspicuous, partially hidden by a row of potted ferns, but where I could command a view of most of the waiting room. It was just possible that Edward might have taken the next train, or contacted some agent, though I wasn't sure what to look for in that case. Some sort of Pinkerton man, scrutinizing faces.

We got aboard the train without incident, though the porter was grouchy about accommodating our "rather large" trunks to the "rather small" Pullman room. In fact it was no real problem—Daniel was so excited about his magazines that he could have read them standing up, so having to sit on the trunk was no burden.

I got little enough reading done myself, since Daniel had to read out to me every stirring passage about Dodge City. I could have listened to him babbling on about anything, though, forever, so full of pity and love I was and so relieved at our escape.

We had an adequate meal of roast chicken in the dining car, seated with two traveling men who extolled the virtues of their lines of shoes and bicycles. The bicycle man was actually interesting, and on my request repaired back to his seat to fetch me a brochure.

Daniel had grown through two bicycles in Philadelphia, the large-wheeled penny-farthings that nowadays you only see in museums and parades. The "safety" bicycles this man was promoting looked much more practical, and he assured us they were much simpler to ride—the difference between riding a horse and being drawn in a carriage.

He was a funny man; he blushed and turned his eyes away from me when he spoke—and thought—about my riding a horse or bicycle. I suppose I might have blushed in return, though I had never as an adult straddled a horse. I rode, but had an old-fashioned sidesaddle. I supposed that would be mirth-provoking in Kansas.

Both of us were intrigued by the pictures, and I resolved to order one once I was established in a job, providing that whatever passed for roads in Dodge City would accommodate such a machine. The salesman claimed he could deliver a bicycle anywhere in the country—so long as it had a rail stop—within two weeks. It was exciting, mainly for Daniel, but I also liked the idea of being independent of horses and carriages. Some of the pictures in the brochure showed women gaily riding along, though I wasn't sure how one could mount the machine without exposing a certain amount of ankle, or worse.

I slept that night better than I had in years, free of Edward and rocked by the motion of the train.

Daniel hardly slept at all, thanks to the small electric light over his bunk. It was probably as much the novelty of being allowed to stay up and read as it was the drama of the stories he was reading.

The train stopped several times during the night, but I didn't wake until dawn, when we began laboring up the final hills through the "Black Country," around Latrobe, to Pittsburgh. I suppose Daniel fell asleep about then; he was too groggy to go to the dining car for breakfast. I brought him back toast and tea, but they went to waste.

The blast furnaces were darkening the sky again, after the strikes and depression, and Pittsburgh seemed both modern and monstrous. I was glad we were only to spend a few hours there. The porter helped us unload and I left Daniel to "guard" our trunks, by sleeping on them. In the coffee shop I wrote a short letter to Edward, and copied it into my diary:

June 25th, 1894

Edward:
   God may one day forgive you for what you did to our son, but I never will. I have taken him away from your vileness forever.
   Don't try to contact us or find us. I will take

*you straight to court and expose you for the mon-
ster you are. It is only for Daniel's sake that I
didn't do so in the process of divorce.*

*If Daniel wants to go to you after he is an
adult, I cannot stop him. Until then, I will keep
him safe from you, and pray that God remove you
from this Earth.*

It was difficult for me to write the word *divorce,*
and I was not sure that I was sincere in the threat. It
seems odd to me now, and weak, but to me the marriage vow was absolute, a life sentence.

I was not young then, but naive, in spite of education. It's quite clear to me now that instead of running off to Kansas, I should have walked into the law
offices of the proper Victorian gentlemen who conducted Edward's affairs, told them what had happened, and found out what the price would be for
divorce in return for silence. I suspect Daniel and I
would have had our independence easily, relocating
with a comfortable sum or income. Instead of the
strange journey.

Perhaps God ordains these things. The world
would be much different now, if I had acted more
rationally. Millions of people now living would be
dead, or unborn.

We are "derailed."

We hadn't planned to spend more than a day in Buffalo, but the larger world of politics and labor stepped in.

I had not been following the news. Our Pullman cars were the invention and property of George Pullman, who had built a city outside Chicago, a "company town," named after himself. He had reduced wages over the winter, to save jobs, supposedly—but he didn't reduce the rent his workers had to pay in the town of Pullman. There was some rabble-rousing, and ultimately almost all of the workers joined the ARU, American Railway Union, and went on strike.

When we got to Buffalo on June 26th, the ticket-master wasn't able to give me a ticket on to Cincinnati, because there was a strike against any line handling Pullman equipment.

The newspaper only had a small story about it, crowded out by the shocking news from France: President Carnot was assassinated, stabbed to death in his own carriage by an Italian anarchist. There was also a story about a terrible tornado in Kansas, which made me apprehensive but filled Daniel with perverse glee.

There was no telling how long the strike would go on. I investigated two alternatives: proceeding west via Canadian rails (the Grand Trunk Railway was slow but not on strike) or taking a steamboat up the Great Lakes. We decided on the latter course, although it did mean waiting for a couple of days, with the sudden demand on the steamship line by businessmen as well as tourists.

It occurred to me also that a customs declaration, upon entering Canada and returning, could give Edward too much information about our whereabouts. My letter might not frighten him, but rather spur him to action.

We took advantage of the delay and spent a day touring Niagara Falls, beautiful but, for me, terrifying. At Daniel's insistence I had agreed to visit the Cave of the Winds, which turned out to be a little too exciting. Baedeker's says "only those of strong nerves should attempt the trip through the Cave of the Winds, which, however, is said to be safe and is often made by ladies." There were no other ladies in our group; I had to hold the hand of a gentleman stranger, as well as my son's, as we sidled along a narrow path with our noses against the rock cliff and the unending explosion of the huge cascade at our backs.

Other than that experience, the falls lived up to their reputation as one of God's great wonders, although the constant importunings of merchants were annoying, and in context seemed almost sacrilegious. In the deafening roar at the base of the falls, people would tug on your sleeve and shout, trying to sell you a postal card or souvenir fan.

In Buffalo, we stayed at the Niagara Hotel, a sumptuous place that cost five dollars a night. (To put that into modern perspective, my notes show that the steamboat ride all the way to Chicago was only twenty dollars, including berth and all meals for almost a week.)

I enjoyed touring the city by electric tramway,

though Daniel was disgusted by the lack of excitement—we should have done Buffalo the first day and Niagara the second. He *was* impressed by a mile-long block of coal elevators twenty stories tall, seeing little service due to the strike. I most remember the public library, surprisingly large and dignified, with a good art collection and a room of literary curiosities, including Edgar Allan Poe's watch, which impressed me because of "The Tell-Tale Heart."

The steamboat left about sundown, and although it proved reasonably comfortable except for the noise and occasional smoke on deck, it was grindingly slow and tedious compared to rail travel. Daniel taught me how to play cribbage, and we traded vast sums in ersatz IOU's.

The parlor aboard the boat had an ample collection of railway schedules, though of course there was no sure way of knowing which ones were closed down by the strike. Daniel and I sorted through the collection, writing down possible routes that did not advertise Pullman service, and presumably would not be affected by the strike.

Studying the large map on the wall, though, I had a sudden inspiration. For an extra five dollars, we could continue via steamer avoiding Chicago altogether to Duluth, and from there entrain to St. Paul,

Minnesota (the Minneapolis–St. Paul & Duluth Railroad didn't have Pullmans, being only 151 miles in extent). St. Paul was the northern terminus of the Diamond Jo Line of steamers, which plied the Mississippi.

We were both excited by the idea of going down Mark Twain's river! I had read *Huckleberry Finn* to Daniel as a bedtime story when he was seven and eight, and had myself read the original *Life on the Mississippi*—though if I'd seen the later, sadder version of that book, I might have been less enthusiastic.

(It occurs to me that I should remind modern readers that in 1894 the age of the steamboat was well past. The train from New York to Chicago cost less and only took a day. Old people took steamships out of nostalgia—or fear of "railroad spine"—but to most, it was an eccentric mode of transportation that one might use for a day or so of sightseeing, or as a change of pace from a long railroad journey.)

Our cabin was small but pleasant, and we slept well after a day of running around; I also felt a new sense of security for the time being—Edward might have people watching railroad stations, but there was no one on his side who could walk on water!

I woke in time to see the sunrise over Erie's picturesque harbor. After a hearty breakfast, we took the air in the ship's bow as it moved swiftly along close to shore, dense woodlands going by, with many deer and birds ignoring us. We congratulated ourselves on our decision; it seemed a most agreeable way to travel. By Friday we would be singing a different tune.

Cleveland looked serene and beautiful from the water. We docked at about four and were advised to go ashore for supper. With directions from the porter, we went a few blocks to the Stillman Hotel, where we had lake fish so delicate and superb I can still recall the flavor.

City quickly gave way to forest as we plied on into the dark. We looked at the stars for a while—I reviewed the major constellations with Daniel, who had a talent for seeing fanciful shapes in the sky. I remember him insisting that Draco was President Cleveland riding a giraffe.

The next day was a lazy one; I drew and painted while Daniel played with some boys his age. I smelled tobacco on his breath and chastised him for it—did he want his father's cough?—which made him sulk, but he recovered as we moved up the Detroit River, and traffic became varied and interesting. We passed a long barge ferrying a locomotive with twenty-two cars.

We slept through the loading and unloading at

Detroit, but woke at Port Huron. Our boat passed over the new train tunnel connecting the United States and Canada, a prodigy of engineering—a cast-iron tube wider than a locomotive and more than a mile long. I was glad to be over it rather than in it.

The gray sky darkened as we went slowly through a narrow strait, and when it opened out into Lake Huron, the rain and wind began. The steamboat charged on into the storm, slapping against waves with a slow rise and jarring fall, meanwhile rocking from side to side in the wind.

Both of us were violently ill. Our belongings slid and crashed around the cabin. The porter came around to tell us not to light any lamps, and I asked him whether there was any relief for our seasickness. He directed me to the infirmary, where I had to wait in a miserable line to purchase a bottle of medicine, a solution of menthol and cocaine in alcohol.

It worked a lot better for Daniel than for me. He was soon snoring in bed. The medicine did quiet my stomach, but seemed to excite my other sensibilities. I spent hours staring out at the roiling waves frozen in the flashbulb thrusts of lightning, gripped by an unnatural state between fear and wonder.

The feeling of being transported to another plane was so extreme that it frightened me deeply, as if I were facing death—even though I was aware that it was the medicine affecting my brain, coupled with purely understandable fear of the storm and anxiety over Daniel's safety and Edward's malevolence. I felt profoundly forsaken by God, as I never had before in my life.

In later years I could see a reason for this so necessary trial, and wonder at the ingenuity of Fate—God's tool, or servant, or master—in providing an earthly foretaste of my unearthly destiny.

The storm ebbed at about three in the morning, and I fell into an exhausted sleep. I woke at dawn to the hooting of an owl—my diary says "the moping owl does to the moon complain," from a poem in Palgrave's—and we were in the calm harbor of Detour, a small fishing and logging village.

Daniel woke famished and he had a good breakfast (I managed a pot of tea and some dry crackers) while we steamed up a lovely river, the St. Marys. In a couple of hours we arrived at Sault-Ste.-Marie, where we were to transfer to the Chicago steamer.

I was ready to spend a day on dry land, so we arranged for a stayover and moved our belongings into the Iroquois Hotel. Daniel was immediately seduced by a handbill advertising "Shoot the Rapids with an Indian Guide!" I enquired at the desk and the bell captain said it was thrilling but perfectly safe. At three dollars, it cost as much as our room, but I was in no mood to be parsimonious, or to seem overly protective. Daniel loved canoeing and was very good at it, so we took a landau up to the head of the Soo Rapids, where I left him in the care of a young Indian man, gruff but with a sparkle in his eye. The landau then took me down to the take-out point at the bottom of the rapids, where it would return in two hours. Those two hours would profoundly change our lives.

Daniel was probably ecstatic to be away from Mother for awhile, but I of course was apprehensive, not so much because he was hurtling down a foaming stream under the guidance of a savage stranger, as just for the simple fact of his being out of my sight for the first time since we had fled.

Hunger distracted me; the smell of a wood fire and roasting fish. Indian men were standing in the water, scooping whitefish out of the stream with nets—I supposed the poor fish were dazed from threading their way through the rapids!—and women were cleaning the fish and pegging them to planks, to roast by the open fire.

I bought a plate of fish and took it with a cup of cool water to a table shaded by an awning. There was a woman sitting there reading the Bible, making notes on the pages with a pencil. That made me uneasy; as a child, I was told that writing in a Bible was sacrilege, and although I had come to feel that that was misdirected piety, I had never gone so far as to write in a Bible myself.

"Oh, the fish is ready!" she said, and put the book aside. She went to the fire and got a plate and returned, sampling it daintily as she walked.

She sat across from me. "You're not from around here."

I extended my hand. "Rosanne Libby" (the name I'd been using for travel) "Philadelphia, born in Georgia." I didn't try to hide my slight accent.

She cocked her head. "After the war."

"No, I'm a little older than that. My parents sent me north just before it began."

She squeezed my hand. "I'm sorry." She shook her head. "You lost them."

"A long time ago."

"Long." She toyed with a piece of fish. "My father died at Shiloh. I barely remember him; I was only two."

"I was three when I left them. They lived a few years, until Sherman took Atlanta."

"Have you forgiven them? The Northerners?"

"I *am* a Northerner." An odd conversation, the first one I'd had with an adult in a week. "The ones who killed my parents . . ."

"What of them?" she said quietly.

There was something in her nature that compelled truthfulness. "I take comfort in knowing that they burn in hell, or will soon."

"Do I know . . . I do know how you feel." She sprinkled salt on her fish. "I'm Toba Bacharach. I'm a minister here."

"Truly!" That was not common in the nineties.

"A missionary, actually, to the Indians. So I'm an expert when it comes to bitterness."

I took a pinch of salt and rubbed it over my plate. "So how do you feel about the Rebels? The ones at Shiloh?"

"Sometimes I hope they found Jesus, and their sins were washed clean.

"Other times?"

She smiled. "I'm a terrible sinner, too. In fact, I sometimes hope they drank and gambled"—she covered her mouth—"and took pleasure where they might. And then were surprised to wake up in hell-fire."

I had to laugh. "I never thought it through so elaborately."

"Then you must not be a minister. We're thorough."

"No, schoolteacher." I took a deep breath: God forgive me, the first person I was to tell the whole lie to had to be a minister! "My husband passed away last year—"

"Oh—I'm so sorry!"

"He was . . . never well. I couldn't stay in Philadelphia; there are too many memories there. So I decided to come out west, to Kansas, where teachers are in demand. My fourteen-year-old son was very much in favor of the idea."

She nodded, smiling. "Boys. He talked you into letting him do the rapids."

"He's persuasive. Should I have said no?"

"No, it's perfectly safe. I know both the boys who act as guides. They've done it so often it bores them to distraction."

"Not too distracted, I hope."

"No." She smiled. "But they do have a strange way about them. It's as if they were dreaming, though they steer the boats quickly, with precision. They say the river talks to them."

"That makes sense," I said. "As metaphor, at least."

Her eyebrows went up, then down. I'd revealed more education than a schoolmarm needed. "No, not at all; not to them. The river is as real a person as you or me. It talks and they listen." In a drawing room in Philadelphia, this would have been an opportunity to bring up Ruskin and his pathetic fallacy. Instead, I nodded.

"Everything has a spirit to them. The river, the rocks, the trees." She carefully extracted the backbone and ribs from her fish. "The fish, the deer, the sun and stars. It makes preaching to them difficult." She shook her head, smiling. "Last Sunday we wrestled with the idea of the Trinity. One God with three aspects. They thought that was funny—only *three?*"

I followed her example with the bones. "They have a point."

"But really. They're so simple. Drives me mad." She was hungry for an audience—her husband, also a preacher, refused to talk about her work with the Indians, thinking it a total waste of time. After an hour, I had some sympathy with him. They were an obstinate bunch, who apparently saw Sunday school as a source of amusement and pastry.

But she planted a seed in my mind, which would germinate in Kansas, and later, in Alaska, grow and flower. And one terrible night, it would save my life, and give me new worlds.

The first threat.

Daniel emerged from the canoe ride drenched and excited. He would have gone back and done it again if I'd let him. I was concerned with money and time and getting him into some dry clothes. I didn't find out until the next day that the canoe had overturned, and he and the Indian, Sam, had swum to shore and then raced down the riverbank to retrieve it! He'd wanted to repeat the adventure to see whether they could make it around that particular bend without capsizing again. Boys!

Our steamer for the two-day trip to Duluth was small and shabby, but Daniel was happy because we were compelled to take separate berths, he in a males-only section, where he had plenty of boisterous company. None of the other boys had "done" the rapids.

I actually had a fine time myself. There had been a pretty good bookstore in Soo, and I'd gotten two used Sherlock Holmes books and Stevenson's novel *The Master of Ballantrae* (plus another Stevenson for Daniel's birthday). It was not only my reading that was fantastic—the first afternoon we passed a long geological formation called Pictured Rocks, sandstone in every color of the rainbow, carved by the elements into impossible shapes. I did a watercolor sketch which, although reasonably accurate, looked like a work of purest imagination. A few years after the War, I saw an exhibition of Salvador Dalí, and his tortured landscapes took me back there to the shores off Lake Superior.

(That means World War II, for the benefit of readers at the other end of this ink-driven time machine. For the first half of my life, "the War" meant the War Between the States, but the phrase's meaning has changed three times since. I can hope that Korea doesn't become World War III, and thence "the War" for its own tenure, but hope is in short supply right now.)

Lake Superior was as placid as Huron had been rough, the nights cold for late June, but we had quilts and entertainment in the small lounge, from some of the passengers—a family of gospel singers and a man who was rather their opposite, a ragtime piano player who reeked of whiskey. He played with precision but could hardly walk without assistance.

We weren't following the news, but as it turned out, we were fortunate to have bypassed Chicago. The Pullman strikers and their sympathizers started to set fires and battle with the police and the Illinois National Guard. President Cleveland eventually sent in half the U.S. Army; pictures of downtown looked like an armed camp.

The harbor at Duluth was clogged with waiting barges, stalled by the strike. A sign proclaimed it "The Zenith City of the Unsalted Seas," and on normal days it was probably full of industry and bustle. Our steamer had to maneuver back and forth, bumping against the closely anchored barges, to find its way to the passenger wharf.

I was afraid we also might be stuck in Duluth for the duration of the strike, but there was no problem:

the Minneapolis–St. Paul & Duluth Railroad didn't have any Pullman equipment. In fact, there was a train leaving in less than an hour from when we arrived at the station.

No time for supper, so I bought two "box meals" from a merchant at the station, along with bottles of chilled root beer, wrapped up in sheets of old newspapers to stay cool for the trip.

I didn't have too much appetite, as it turned out. The car was crowded and Daniel had to stand most of the way. My sex earned me a hard padded seat, covered with straw weaving that had decayed beyond function. Breathing was difficult, the air blue with cigar and pipe smoke. Even less appetizing were the men who took their tobacco in oral form, spitting wherever they pleased.

It was faster than the boat, something we had been looking forward to, but there was little else to recommend it for five hours. A blur of dense forest became a blur of cornfields. Just before St. Paul, we stopped at two beautiful lakes, resort areas, and enough people got off so that Daniel could find a seat. He was worn out and immediately fell asleep with his head on my shoulder.

There was an unpleasant surprise waiting at the St. Paul station. Leaving Daniel with the bags, I went toward the information desk, and stopped dead at a corkboard that said MESSAGES FOR TRANSIENTS. There were columns of envelopes in alphabetical order, and one of them had my name on it.

I was paralyzed by a whirlwind of conflicting emotions. He couldn't know where we were—or could he? Most likely, he had sent messages to be posted at every major railway station.

Would he be notified if I took the envelope? Even if he were, how could he know it was me, rather than some idler intent on other people's business? No one was overseeing the message board.

Nothing he could say would make any difference. I should have just left it there—but then I would have been obsessed by it for weeks or months. Finally, I strode over and snatched it. It might reveal whether he knew anything about our progress.

The envelope was sealed, unfortunately; otherwise I might have taken a peek and returned it. I slit the top of the envelope with a penknife, and found a short note in a stranger's hand:

> *Rec'd by telegraph 8:05 P.M. June 24th: You must know by now that what you have done is both irrational and illegal. Return at once, and nothing will be said about it. If you force me to*

take action, it will be hard on both you and the boy.

There is no place you can go where I won't find you. Do not delude yourself about that. The longer you try to hide, the harder it will be on you. Edward.

I glanced over at Daniel and saw he was fast asleep, draped protectively over our luggage. Nobody seemed to be looking at me. I slipped the note into my purse and returned the envelope to its place. You couldn't tell from the front that it had been opened.

We found a comfortable room in the Ryan, not far from the station, which I took under yet another assumed name. Daniel accepted the change without question. I didn't tell him about the note from his father. I copied it into my diary while he slept, and then threw it away, which was improvident. It would have been interesting evidence if we came to legal proceedings.

The next sailing for St. Louis was two days away, which was all right for me. I didn't want to immediately board the boat that we'd be stuck on for seven hundred miles. We spent the next day wandering around St. Paul, which was more pleasant than I'd expected. The city had an all-electric tramway that only cost a nickel (a tenth the cost of the short cab ride to the hotel). We climbed to the top of the capitol dome, which was arduous but resulted in a splendid view. Having seen Minneapolis in the distance, we resolved to have lunch there, so we took the interurban tram, also electric, over the Mississippi.

(That was an hour each way, but it was pleasant—especially compared to the railroad—bright and well ventilated, the gentlemen using spittoons or the open window. I read much of the time, having brought the Stevenson and a new copy of *Life on the Mississippi,* its garish board covers and cheap saffron paper a stark contrast to the leather-and-vellum edition I'd read from Edward's library.)

We spent the afternoon out at the Indian Mounds, where Daniel went off on a fruitless search for arrowheads, while I sat at Carver's Cave and attempted a drawing that was no more successful. Dinner at the hotel café, and early to bed.

The age of the steamboat, as I've said, was long past. This is how Mark Twain put it in 1883, eleven years before our voyage:

> *Mississippi steamboating was born about 1812; at the end of thirty years it had grown to mighty proportions, and in less than thirty years, it was*

dead! A strangely short life for so majestic a crea-
ture. Of course it is not absolutely dead; neither is
a crippled octogenarian who could once jump
twenty-two feet on level ground; but as contrasted
with what it was in its prime vigor, Mississippi
steamboating may be called dead.

We boarded the *Davenport* after breakfast, and I was relieved to find it a clean and apparently well maintained vessel. The captain and several others wore blue uniforms with sharp creases and lots of shiny brass.

Two boys younger than Daniel were engaged in tacking up bunting of red, white, and blue, as it was July 4th. We asked if there would be fireworks, and got the obvious answer: "Aboard a *boat?* I should hope not!"

Our room was small and close but clean, and had a window that could be opened partway. At precisely nine, the whistle shrieked, and we departed with surprising speed. Daniel ran off to explore the boat. I looked in the lounge, but it was full of loud men smoking and drinking coffee, so I went on up to the very top, the "hurricane" deck. It was quite fresh; I had to go back to the cabin for a wrap.

Coming back up, I glimpsed Daniel in the lounge,

puffing on a cigarillo. I resolved not to be so much of an old hen about it. The effect on his body probably bothered me less than the resemblance to his father it gave him.

We passed under four or five bridges on the way out of St. Paul. The scenery was engaging, but soon I was totally absorbed in rereading the Mark Twain book, in this most appropriate of settings.

One of the boys brought me a pot of tea, and I was comfortable on a fabric folding chair, tea and book on a table in front of me. After awhile, a handsome man sat down across from me and attempted to start up a conversation. He was about my age, but wore old-fashioned muttonchops and a big flowing moustache. Rather like Mark Twain, actually.

He was probably an interesting man, but of course that was not a complication I needed at the time. I rebuffed him, less gently than I should have. In the safety of my own parlor, I would have enjoyed chatting and even flirting with him. But the *Davenport* was a small space to share with a few dozen men for four days. I would be a virtuous married woman, avoiding even the appearance of sin, and that was how I presented myself to the old-fashioned man. He left with a perplexed expression, and a few minutes later I realized he might have been talking to

Daniel downstairs, who would have been faithful to our cover story of widowhood.

Toward noon, two men in white set up a large folding table and covered it with a starched white cloth. They brought up a large sliced ham and a dark brown smoked turkey, and then platters of bread and cakes and bowls of fruit. Finally, a huge punch bowl with a block of ice, into which they poured several pitchers of cider, some sliced-up lemons and oranges, and two jugs of what smelled like pure alcohol. Meanwhile, someone below rang a loud tinkling bell, like a triangle, and shouted "Come and get it!"

I guess the stairway had been closed off during the preparations, which was why I'd had the hurricane deck to myself for an hour. Now a whole crowd surged up, laughing and chattering. The two young boys struggled up behind them, lugging a washtub full of iced-down bottled drinks. I was glad to see Daniel was helping them; not so glad to see him take a beer from the tub when they set it down. He looked at me warily, and I said one was all right, for the Fourth. Just don't go near that punch.

The pilot came up to carve the turkey and tell a few stories: progressively less believable tall tales. The only other unescorted ladies, two German girls and a pinch-faced old maid, sat down at my table. The old woman introduced herself as Miss Stroff, and then began to knit with furious concentration. I speak no German, but the girls and I were able to hold a simple conversation in French.

They had gone more than halfway around the world! Sisters, they had left Munich with their father after their mother's death a few years before. He had gone to Kowloon, China, working with a tea export concern, and then moved on to California after that enterprise failed. They lived in a German enclave, Sutter's Mill, while their father worked at a small gold mine. It was hard work and more dangerous than they knew; he apparently died of progressive arsenic poisoning.

For most of a year they'd worked as domestics for a wealthy German family, eking out their income with "gifts from gentlemen," until they had saved enough to return to Germany. Prostitutes! They blushed and looked at the floor upon admitting this. I was truly at a loss for words. (The old woman, who before had given no sign of being able to speak French, gasped and left the table.)

They were headed for New York to take a steamer across, but the Pullman strike stranded them. Then they found it would be less expensive to go down the Mississippi and proceed directly from New Orleans to Europe. I was sure they were misinformed about that, but kept my own counsel. They were committed to this course, and it was obvious in their voices that they had to leave this horrible place, America, and seek a normal life in Germany.

A gunshot frightened all of us, but it was followed immediately by laughter, and then a fusillade. Some men in the bow, below, were shooting at a floating bottle. That became the main entertainment for the afternoon. Someone brought out a fowling piece, even louder than the revolvers, to shoot at bottles in midair. If anybody else was bothered by increasingly pixilated men firing weapons every which way, they didn't show it. I spent a lot of time in my cabin, reading what would be one of the most important books of my life.

The German girls had read a lot of French literature, and I had read a bit. The elder one had just finished a novel by Camille Flammarion, whom I knew not as a novelist but as a science writer. Just a few months before, I had read his new *Popular Astronomy,* from the Philadelphia library, in English translation.

She loaned me the novel, *Lumen,* which I took downstairs (tolerating the heat better than the noise and danger) and read with some difficulty but with increasing fascination. It was about a man on Earth who is able to talk with a spirit creature who roams from world to world, in space.

It's worth noting for modern readers that in those days, before it had been proven that the moon and Mars were lifeless, the idea of life on other worlds was not at all fantastic. The astronomy books that I read at Wellesley generally assumed that most or even all of the planets were inhabited. But this French novel made it seem quite real.

I went back up to the hurricane deck for some supper and found Daniel quite woozy and giggly. He had obviously gotten into the punch or some such libation. I couldn't be too stern with him, since after all I should have been keeping an eye on him rather than reading. But I sent him down to the cabin to nap, saying I would come get him if there were fireworks.

The shooting had stopped, so I sat out on the foredeck to read, while the sour old lady knitted away silently. Perhaps influenced by the book, I noted in my diary that the sunset had an unearthly beauty, the cloudless sky going from lemon-yellow to crimson, the moon a barely visible fingernail paring, diving after the sun. I wondered what sunsets would be like on worlds like Jupiter, which, I knew from the telescope at school, had skies already full of color, and many large moons.

I roused Daniel, only a little groggy, because the pilot had said we'd be passing Wabasha as it got dark, and they'd certainly have some sort of display.

While we waited I told him all about the Flammarion book, and he was pretty excited until I admitted that it was in French, not his favorite subject. He'd liked the language so little he'd switched to Latin. He did much better in it than his mother had.

Indeed there were fireworks, and although they were some miles away, that in itself was a little exotic and charming. Instead of being in the middle of them, we were distant observers, the faint popping sounds seemingly random, unassociated with the bursts of sparks and stars.

Of course the gentlemen had to unleash their revolvers and fire them into the air, in accompaniment. It's a good thing we weren't in any danger from savage Indians. Our gallant protectors would run out of ammunition and we'd all be scalped.

I read until past midnight, sipping a little more sherry than I was accustomed to. I had a strange and compelling dream, strong and odd enough for me to mention it in the next day's diary entry. More than fifty years later, I'm struck by the element of prophecy in it: *I dreamed that an unearthly creature, whose shape was indistinct, took me to worlds that were dreams*

within a dream. I knew I was dreaming, but that dream
partook of a strange reality, as did the dream within it.

I had a headache the next day bad enough to keep
me in bed until noon. I was grateful that there was no
more gunplay; maybe the men who had been up all
night doing it were in no better condition than me.

Daniel slept late but otherwise seemed not to
show any aftereffects from his excesses. He went out
for breakfast and brought me back some salicylate of
soda, which the cook was selling in penny packets. I
drank it down with a pint of cool water, and my condition did improve. When I went up for a bowl of
soup I was treated to the sight of Trempealeau Island,
five hundred feet high and most beautiful.

The fifth was Daniel's birthday. I found him up
on the hurricane deck, reading a week-old newspaper, and gave him his present: Stevenson's *The Strange
Case of Dr. Jekyll and Mr. Hyde*. He devoured it in one
long sitting, and for years it was his favorite book. I
later read it, though, and wondered whether it might
have been too horrific for a boy his age. If somebody
had told me that in my later years I would be writing
equally horrific, if less literary, tales, for a penny a
word, I would have scoffed.

For all that day and the next, I worked my way
through the Flammarion book, making a list of words

and phrases I couldn't puzzle out, along with their page numbers. Greta and Valerie were glad to sit with me and try to translate—Greta especially, because the book aroused in her the same fascination it did in me.

Many years later, I regretted not being able to talk with them frankly about their lives in California. Today I could; it's hard to shock an old woman. They were apparently lighthearted and casual about it, and I might have learned things from them that would have made that aspect of marriage easier. My main concern at the time, though (other than the Flammarion book), was keeping Daniel away from them. He was a pretty lad, and had what I now admit were normal impulses for a fourteen-year-old. To me at the time, he was still a vulnerable child, and I his only protector—and the pain his father had caused both of us did nothing to liberalize my attitude toward carnality.

New worlds.

After I returned the book to them, I wrote down this:
Flammarion makes it seem not just likely, but in-
evitable, that other worlds should be inhabitable. To
deny that is almost impious, saying that God's powers of
creation are finite. The people on those worlds must be
wondrous indeed, evolving to adapt to their harsh and
bizarre conditions. (Darwin's *Origin of Species* was
published the year after I was born, and when I was
in college it was part of the canon, though still fod-
der for righteously indignant sermons.)

When we passed by Hannibal, the pilot entertained us after dinner with an hour's reading from Twain's book. He was a natural comedian, and did the voices of the querulous and gruff in a way that had us helpless with laughter.

The next day, though, we had cause to wonder why they call this river the Mississippi rather than the Missouri. We reached the confluence of the two, and it was obvious that the rich muddy waters of the Missouri quite overwhelmed the northern "branch." For many miles the two ran in parallel courses, until the clear Mississippi finally blended with its turbid sister.

Then we came to the end of the line for Diamond Jo Steamers, St. Louis. It was strange to be on land again after so many days. Both of us found that if we tried to stand still, the ground would continue to rock under our feet, a disturbing sensation that lasted at least a whole day.

We took a room at the Planter's Hotel, and Daniel tagged along while I went off to shop for another working dress. I was able to leave him in a bookstore while I was being fitted.

I'd found out that the Missouri Pacific Railroad had put on an early-morning train, without sleepers, to Kansas City, so we came down to the station at six thirty the next morning. There were a hundred or so people slumped around the waiting room, not all of us in sympathy with the Pullman strikers.

The trip to Kansas City was uneventful. We back-tracked a bit, going along the Missouri River all morning, and then went off into the featureless plains after Jefferson City. The porter gave us a deck of cards, and Daniel, with undisguised avidity, taught me how to play poker, which he had picked up on the steamboat while I was immersed in Flammarion. We played for toothpicks, and after a couple of hours he had almost all of them—and then I mastered the idea of bluffing, and won almost all of them back. What kind of mother would lie to her son over a couple of toothpicks?

It did pass the time, but we were both tired and sore by the time we got to Kansas City at sundown. We could have continued down into Kansas (K.C. is in Missouri) but decided to rest up. We got a shabby but clean room at the Centropolis.

I thought about suggesting to Daniel that we come to ground here. Kansas City was probably the last place we would see that would have anything like the amenities we were accustomed to. But the aim of our flight was to wind up at "the ends of the earth," where Edward would never find us. And I harbored the hope that after we had hidden out for a few years, we might return to civilization, east or west.

We rested for a day, strolling. We crossed the bridge over to Kansas City, Kansas. The smell of the stock-yards and packing-houses could turn one into a veg-etarian.

I went into several pawnshops in both Missouri and Kansas, having my wedding ring appraised. One of the Missouri ones offered $250, fifty dollars more than anybody else, so I took it back there and sold it. I suppose it was worth twice as much, at least, but I was glad to be rid of it. The ruby necklace I had traded a tooth for brought another hundred.

The next day, we boarded the morning train to Topeka, where we picked up the branch to Dodge City.

Miles and miles of grain, and then desolate, un-tamed prairie from horizon to horizon. Daniel stared out the window for hours on end, ignoring the book in his lap. I let him be. He had probably expected something more interesting.

A few years before, Dodge City had been the epit-ome of the wild and wooly west. The town literally started as a saloon. Fort Dodge had been in place since 1865, an outpost that protected pioneers on the

Santa Fe Trail. In 1872, a Canadian named George Hoover showed up with a wagonload of whiskey, knowing that liquor was not allowed within five miles of the fort. He measured out five miles down the trail, set up a tent, and made a bar out of a board and two stacks of sod. That became the town.

There's a popular radio show now, *Gunsmoke,* that purports to be about Dodge City in the early days, but it's far too wholesome. The town had two periods of prosperity. The first one was from 1872 to 1876, when the town was called Buffalo City, and was the West's main shipping point for buffalo hides and meat. Millions of the animals were killed by men who essentially sat in one place and shot them like fish in a barrel, until they were exterminated.

It was a very rough town then. Seventeen people were killed in shoot-outs the first year of its existence, most in the "no man's land" south of the railroad tracks. North of the tracks, even then, it was illegal to carry a gun.

Dodge might have died with the buffaloes if not for a legislative action that made it "Queen of the Cowtowns," a dubious distinction. Texas longhorns used to be driven every year to railheads in Abilene, Ellsworth, and Wichita—but it turned out the Texas cows were killing the Kansas ones. They carried a tick to which they were immune, but which caused a killing fever in the local cattle.

The Kansas legislature established a quarantine line that protected those three cities, and by default gifted Dodge with the annual visit of a quarter of a million tick-infested cattle. Along with the cows came cowboys, of course—and gunmen, card sharps, prostitutes, and whoever else might make a dollar off these bored and tired and reckless men.

It only lasted ten years. In 1885, the quarantine was extended to include the whole state. Dodge had its own cattle by then, presumably immune to the tick disease—but the winter of '85/'86 was one long blizzard, which all but destroyed the industry.

When our train pulled into town nine years later, Dodge was still a cowtown without many cows. (I called the Chamber of Commerce in 1951, and they reluctantly admitted that the bovine population was *still* under the 1885 level.) But there were people, and the people had children, and the children needed teachers.

I had hoped to sit down with some frontier rustics and sweep them off their feet with my obvious education, and so be able to continue living under an assumed name and false background—but even in

Dodge, that would not be possible. A schoolteacher had to establish her credentials. So I gave them my real name and they wired Wellesley for my bona fides.

I suspected then that it was only a matter of time before Edward would follow that trace back to Dodge. As it turned out, he would be slow, and we would have more than four years of grace.

Almost sixty years later, I wonder what was in my head. When they asked for my credentials, I should have demurred and put Daniel back on the train, and traveled on, perhaps to Mexico or Central America. Anywhere the law could reach us, a lawyer could as well. For all his faults, Edward was a good lawyer.

And he was not a man to be bested by a woman.

None of that was in my mind when the train pulled away from the depot in Dodge, leaving us alone, tired, dusty, and baking under the Kansas summer sun. There was no one in charge at the depot, just an empty telegraph room, but there was a sign offering rooms for rent up on Central Avenue, with a simple map. With no conveyances in sight, we hoisted our belted-together footlockers and headed up the hill.

It was a rooming house run by a Mrs. Clifton, who was a strange and unpleasant woman, suspicious and querulous. I took two rooms for a month because they were cheap, nine dollars apiece, and we were too tired to go off searching for another place. We had been on the Atchison, Topeka & Santa Fe for more than twenty-four hours, including an interminable wait in Hays City, and of course there were no sleepers. I checked our beds for vermin and, finding nothing macroscopic, gratefully collapsed for all the afternoon and night.

In the morning we had a wholesome breakfast of grease and eggs on hard bread, and set out to explore. Daniel wanted to see Boot Hill, where desperados slightly slow on the draw would wind up, but it wasn't there anymore—in fact, if we'd come four years earlier, I might have wound up teaching over those old graves. The bodies had been relocated to Prairie Grove in 1878, and a schoolhouse was built on the lot. But it burned down in '90, and was still charred rubble when we sought it out.

Daniel was not unprepared for the lack of excitement in Dodge; I'd told him about the sarcastic magazine article I'd read, describing how tame it was now. But still I think he was hoping against hope that some cowboy would come around the corner, all clinking spurs and creaking leather. It never happened. No cows, no cowboys, at least in town.

What did happen was a game of stickball near the ruins of the Boot Hill school. They said they could use another player, so Daniel got to work off some energy while I sat on a bench and contemplated our limited future.

There was no shade. Every tree in Dodge was one that had been brought from the East, transplanted and carefully nurtured. Few public areas had trees then—although an enterprising citizen had planted and cultivated an extensive vegetable garden along the railroad tracks, to demonstrate the land's potential fertility to people who might be lunatic enough to try farming.

I went back to Mrs. Clifton's to take a bath, and when Daniel came in he used the water after me (fairly turning it to mud). When night fell we lit kerosene lamps. There were electric lamps on the street, but the house was not wired—Mrs. Clifton thought electricity was dangerous, and she was probably right, at that time and place. Wooden houses like hers were dry tinderboxes.

The next day I went to the Third Ward School and found the principal, Leroy Roberts. He did have an opening for a college-educated teacher, to teach grades nine through twelve.

It looked like a lot of work for seventy-five dollars per month. I would teach from nine till four, an hour off for lunch, with the day divided into thirty-four segments. It was mostly recitation and memorization. My lesson plan was a three-inch stack of paper in a worn leather portfolio, and I would start work in six weeks.

I'd thought about getting a temporary job before school started, but it was obvious I wouldn't have time. I had a basket full of books as well as the portfolio, and a keen sense of all I'd forgotten in the fifteen years since I'd left college. The prospect of declining Latin verbs again filled me with dread, and since childhood I had never been good with history, the memorization of names and dates. I had luck with the Latin, which was being taught by a specialist, but not with history, which of course was heavily weighted toward the history of Kansas and the West.

Without my asking, Daniel volunteered to go out and find a job till school started, which filled me with pride. He knocked on doors for a day, and got a job at a newspaper, the *Globe Live Stock Journal*, cleaning up and sorting type for a dollar a day.

I opened a bank account with the wedding-ring and necklace money, and stored the seventy-three golden eagles in a safe-deposit box, putting them out of my mind. I wanted to hold on to the hard money for insurance. That turned out to be a wise precaution.

During those frantic six weeks we didn't meet many people. The two other lodgers at Mrs. Clifton's were stiff gentlemen who spoke in monosyllables at breakfast and supper, I think embarrassed by the presence of a woman and child. One worked at William's Variety Story (and he was quite friendly when we showed up as customers); the other was a law clerk.

I did befriend Waylon Marcell, the Methodist minister. I joined the choir and promised to help with Sunday school after regular school settled down. The other choir members were cordial but distant. After a few rehearsals I recognized the plain fact that it was a class and regional conflict; I was an Eastern upper-class woman, and to some of them I might as well have come from China. They did warm up after a few months.

Waylon Marcell would change my life. His church was doing informal missionary work (what we now might call "outreach") with a band of Arapaho families camped outside of town, and he wondered whether I, as an "educated woman," might get through to the women better than he. They just stared at him and made no comment, unlike the men, who enjoyed argument.

I had no luck at the time. But in the winter, huddled around the smoky fire in a tipi on Sunday afternoons, they would ask and answer questions. It would be good training for my future.

The months and years pass.

Teachers today would have a low opinion of the way we taught in the 1890s, but it served the students' needs. I delivered facts to them, and enforced memorization by repetition, and then tested their memories. Authorities nowadays would feel I was stifling their creativity, but in fact we hardly had time to cover the basics.

Many, perhaps most, of the children in Dodge lived on farms, and they had jobs to do in season, which of course could not be put off. I was to find out that attendance was pretty good in the winter, subject to storms, but during planting and harvest I would be lucky to have three-quarters attending at any given day. Not the same three-quarters, either; families were large in those days, and the children would trade off. You had to have sympathy for them, but it didn't make teaching easy. I was in charge of seventy-two students, and keeping track of who had missed which lesson was quite a bookkeeping chore.

It was not easy on Daniel to be the teacher's son. There was taunting and, on a few occasions, fights with the class bullies. My own difficulty, teaching him, was in resisting the natural inclination to favor him—and then resisting the contrary instinct to be too harsh on him, so that he would not seem to be favored. He was a subtle young man, though, and clearly understood the tightrope I was walking.

The work was tiring but curative, like diving into a pool whose waters conferred forgetfulness. Philadelphia was lost in the day-to-day minutiae of teaching and administration.

Daniel was a handful, as any boy would be, growing through his teens. His initial disappointment with Dodge, though, gave way to a kind of worldly status, a big-city bravado. Few of his classmates knew anything of life except on the plains, and Philadelphia was much more exotic to them than Dodge City had been to Daniel.

A couple of months into the school year, and after I started teaching Sunday school, I suddenly realized that I was happier than I had been since college. And more at peace with myself than I had ever been.

Dodge had a history, but it was basically a Midwestern town, and I was finding that I liked the people and the life in that part of the country. I won't pretend that I didn't miss the cultural advantages and sometimes-gay social whirl of Philadelphia, but we did have plays and concerts in Dodge, and truly exuberant parties.

People didn't lock their doors when they went out. If you were short of money, the grocer would let you keep track and pay when you could. If anyone were in trouble—even if he was not particularly liked—his neighbors would join forces to help out.

Part of it must have been shared tribulation. After the hooligans like Bat Masterson and the Earp brothers moved on, Dodge settled into agriculture, chiefly cattle. Then the disastrous blizzard of January '86 buried most of the cows in great shoals of snow, pushing them up against fences, to suffocate and freeze. The next year's drought took care of most of what was left.

So there was a quiet sense of people tempered by trouble, self-reliant but interdependent.

Daniel didn't share my comfort. The restlessness that had made him want Dodge was redirected, in his junior year, to the Yukon, when gold was discovered and thousands of men went north to make easy fortunes, or so they thought.

I wouldn't let him leave school, hoping that he would wake up and see the value of a college education (there was even a college of sorts in Dodge at the time). He was a sullen and dreamy student that last year, but he did stay in school, I think more for my sake than for his own ambition. A different kind of boy would have run away.

Then in his senior year, '97/'98, the newspapers started calling for Spanish blood, beating the drum for Cuban independence. In frozen February, the battleship *Maine* blew up and sank in Havana Bay. The saber-rattling grew more and more intense. Like most of his boy classmates, Daniel wanted to put on a uniform and go teach those Spaniards a thing or two.

Those of us old enough to have had lives shattered by the Civil War—by "Bloody Kansas," in Dodge—were not so enthusiastic about the adventure. War was declared in April, and I forbade him to join the army battalion forming up in Topeka.

We had hot arguments about it, his manly blood aboil against my maternal protectiveness. I had been a mother far longer than he had been a man, though, and I won temporarily.

In July, he would turn eighteen, and be in charge of his own destiny. "What about the Yukon?" I said, desperate, preferring that he face blizzards rather than bullets. He said that it could wait. The gold wasn't going anywhere.

The Fourth of July celebration was frenetic with patriotism and righteous bellicosity, beginning with the description of Theodore Roosevelt's Rough Riders' charge up San Juan Hill on July first. Then came word that the Spanish fleet had been totally destroyed at the Battle of Santiago.

My boy was in agony over the thought that the war might be over before he could get to Cuba. That was my most fervent wish, of course, and for that reason I cheered as loudly as the rest.

The fireworks were to give me nightmares, though. I dreamed I could see Daniel charging bravely through the enemy fusillade. Daniel lying torn and dying, dead, in the Cuban mud.

The next day, at dawn, I gave him one of the golden eagles, but not my blessing, for his birthday. He went down to the station to wait for the first train to Topeka.

Having gone to the safe-deposit box, I suppose the eagles were on my mind. But I had almost forgotten about the raven.

I was watering the newly planted vegetable patch, trudging back and forth from the outdoor pump, when I heard wings beating and was startled to turn and see an oversized raven in my path. I instantly recalled the one who had stopped my flight in Philadelphia.

It hopped twice and said, "No gold."

I think my heart actually stopped. "What?" It couldn't possibly be the same bird.

"No gold," it repeated, and didn't budge as I approached it.

"But I have gold," I said, feeling both moronic and terrified. "In the bank."

"No!" it screeched, and flapped up to eye level. "Gold!"

"What are you? Are you a sign?"

"No gold," it said again, almost quietly. Then it flew a block down the street and perched on the flagpole in front of the bank. "No gold!" loud, twice, and it flew away.

I stood there dumb under the baking sun, watching the bird disappear in the distance. Then I took off my sun hat and doused myself with well water.

I went inside and combed my hair and changed into a church blouse. I had a cup of cool tea and then went down to the bank and put all of the golden eagles into my purse, doubling its weight. At home I put them in a paper bag and hid them in the rice canister. I didn't know what else to do.

When Daniel returned the next afternoon, I was ecstatic to see him not in uniform, but that was only a temporary state. The regiment had accepted him, but told him to go home for a week to "put his affairs in order." I knew better than to suggest that he spend the week reconsidering his decision.

I wasn't thinking clearly myself. Of course he would have to use proper identification to prove he was of age; of course the army would send his name to various authorities, to make sure he wasn't a criminal on the run. Including the Pinkerton Agency.

It took until the seventh for Edward to catch up with us.

We had moved into our own small house a couple

of weeks before, which made all the difference. A large man knocked on the door, and when I started to open it, he pushed his way inside.

"Pinkerton," he said, and showed a badge. "You kidnapped the son of Edward Tolliver."

"I did no such thing." He stepped forward, close enough to touch me, but I stood my ground. "I rescued my son from . . ."

"From what?" he demanded.

Saying the words almost made me vomit. "Sodomy. Incest."

"He said you had fantasies about that. You're a dangerous woman. You belong in jail."

"If I belong in jail," I said, "why don't you have an actual policeman along with you?"

"I have the authority—"

I cut him off. "In fact, why don't you and I go down to the sheriff's office and talk about this? I've known him for some years. We sing in the choir together."

That was the last word of mine he heard. Daniel had crept up behind him with a poker from the fireplace, and brought it down on his head with great force. He fell like a tree, the back of his head spouting blood.

"Daniel!"

"I didn't kill him. At least I don't think so." He turned the man over and put an ear to his chest. "Heart's beating."

My mind was spinning, but I did fasten upon a plan, a mad plan. "Rope. Let's tie him up and gag him. It could buy us enough time to get away."

We didn't have coils of rope lying around the house. The man next door had horses, though, and wasn't home, so Daniel "borrowed" a length of leather strap. We tied the Pinkerton man's hands behind his back, and his feet together, and put a tight gag around his mouth. Then we dragged him to the unused bedroom and Daniel locked him inside by kicking a wedge of wood under the door.

Daniel took his pistol. That would have interesting consequences.

I sent him running down to the station to get a cabriolet while I stuffed our trunks with clothes and then got the golden eagles from their hiding place, whispering a prayer of thanks to the raven.

The stationmaster was curious and concerned; I taught his son and daughter, and since this was Sunday, I would obviously be missing school for a day or more. I asked him to pass on word that I had a sister in Kansas City who'd had a stroke, and would telegraph as soon as I knew what was happening. Later I realized how flimsy that story was; the stationmaster had probably told the Pinkerton man where I lived, and then I suddenly showed up with all my worldly goods. Perhaps he didn't like policemen.

We wanted the first train to anywhere, of course, which meant Hays City, in ninety minutes. Daniel went back to guard the man while I waited at the station. It was only a five-minute bicycle ride for him; he would come as soon as he heard the train's whistle.

He told me he watched the man for an hour and he never moved. I never pressed him about it.

I only booked us through to Kansas City, figuring that we'd be harder to trace if we bought one ticket at a time. Waiting for the train to Hays and K.C., I went through the timetables and made a list.

Denver. San Francisco. Seattle. Sitka. Skagway. My boy would have his dream of the Yukon. Where Edward could never find him.

If the man had freed himself and got a fast horse, he might have caught us waiting in Hays. When we got there, I sat on the bench outside the station, clutching the bag that held his pistol, not sure what I would do if he came riding up full of fury.

At that time of my life, I was not sure whether I would be capable of violence. With the benefit of hindsight, I'm certain that I would have overcome lovingkindness and fear of God, and blown him off his horse, or at least tried. But I was not put to the test. The train pulled up at Hays on time and we started to put on miles.

Our most potent enemy was the telegraph. (It would be years before long-distance telephoning was common in the West.) If the Pinkerton man had gotten free, certainly his first action would have been to wire Kansas City, and have another agent waiting for the train.

That would have been interesting. Daniel had his fantasies about shoot-outs, but they probably didn't involve his mother on a train platform.

Our deception began in Ellsworth, where I was fairly certain we wouldn't be recognized. I sacrificed the tickets to K.C., bought under my married name, and as Vivian and Charles Flammarion we boarded the Union Pacific bound for San Francisco. We had to pay an extra dollar for Daniel's bicycle, but he had read of people using them to get to the goldfields. I doubted that myself, but thought he might be able to sell it for a good profit in Skagway.

Six of the golden eagles got us a sleeper—the Pullman strike a distant memory—and though we were ready to make use of it, the sun finally setting on a rather eventful day, we first went to the dining car, which was a pleasantly stupefying experience. Crisp linen and heavy silver and too much beef and claret—a novelty, since Kansas was technically dry, and female schoolteachers might know where to go for a drink, but they dare not show up there.

We both slept through the change to Mountain Time and the little hamlet of First View, where we might have spied Pike's Peak in the light of the rising sun. It was quite visible when we managed to stagger down to last call for breakfast.

It was a pleasant three days for Daniel—excitement, rather than the anxiety of our first flight west. I treated him as an adult, even to the extent of letting him carry the Pinkerton man's pistol in his coat pocket, though he acceded to my request that he not carry it, or any other sidearm, to the Yukon. We knew enough about the Wild West to know that fools with guns killed other fools with guns, and the safest thing was not to challenge them.

In a way, I was terribly wrong. In the long run . . . well, no human will ever know the long run.

Denver looked interesting, and under other circumstances we might have tarried a day or two there. But we had to be realistic. One of us an accused kidnapper and the other having assaulted a Pinkerton man and, technically, deserted the army. I was reluctant to get off the train until we could lose ourselves in the confusion of Gold Rush San Francisco.

Likewise, we didn't get off at Cheyenne, early the next day, which was the last regular stop for over a thousand miles.

As we rose into the Rockies we were treated hourly to scenes of wondrous beauty. Mountains snow-capped in July. Boiling cataracts a hundred feet below us, as we crawled along trestle bridges that seemed none too substantial.

I couldn't properly enjoy the scenery, for my concern over what might be waiting in San Francisco. Daniel had stopped shaving in an attempt at disguise, but three days' growth wasn't going to make much difference.

Chance favored us the second night. At dinner we were seated with two men, a father and son named Doc and Chuck Coleman, who were also headed for the Yukon. They were better prepared than we, having received two letters from a friend who was already there, and information from provisioners in Seattle.

The Canadian government, they told us, wisely would not allow any prospector to enter the country unless he brought in a year's worth of food, as well as necessities for panning. That's a ton of supplies.

Over coffee, after dinner, I made a copy of the list for Daniel, and later copied it into my diary:

Food

Bacon, 100–200 lbs.—Flour, 400 lbs.—
Dried fruits, 75–100 lbs.—Cornmeal, 50
lbs.—Rice, 20–40 lbs.—Coffee, 10–25 lbs.—
Tea, 5–10 lbs.—Sugar, 25–100 lbs.—Beans,
100 lbs.—Condensed milk, 1 case—Salt,
10–15 lbs.—Pepper, 1 lb.—Rolled oats, 25–50
lbs.—Potatoes, 25–100 lbs.—Butter, 25 cans—
Assorted evaporated meats and vegetables

Equipment

Stove—Gold pan—Granite buckets—Cups &
plates (tin)—Knives, forks, & spoons—Coffee/
teapot—Picks & handles—Saws & chisels—
Hammer & nails—Hatchet—Shovels—
Drawknife—Compass—Frying pan—
Matches—Small assortment of medicines

Clothing

1 heavy mackinaw coat—3 suits heavy under-
wear—2 pairs heavy mackinaw trousers—
1 doz. heavy wool socks—6 heavy wool mit-
tens—2 heavy overshirts—2 pairs rubber

*boots—2 pairs heavy shoes—3 pairs heavy
blankets—2 rubber blankets—4 towels—
2 pairs overalls—1 suit oil clothing—Assorted
summer clothing*

They said you could buy an outfit all assembled for around a thousand dollars, but you could save money and probably get better quality if you shopped around, which was what they planned to do.

Daniel stared at the list. "You can't carry all this stuff from the boat to the goldfields on your back."

"Some do, partway," Doc said. "About a hundred pounds at a time, maybe more on a sledge. You go up a ways and start piling it up, and go back for another hundred pounds. When you've got it all piled up in the new place, you start over." He laughed at Daniel's expression. "Not all the way. You get to the Yukon River and build a raft, and let the current take you to Dawson."

"Won't somebody steal your stuff while you're going back and forth?"

"Heared not. I suspect it goes hard on someone who gets caught. Besides, everyone has about the same stuff anyhow."

"We're hoping to get mules, too," Chuck said. "They have lots of them in Skagway."

"Depending on what they cost. We don't want to be flat when we get to the fields." He gave his son a look that bespoke past arguments. "Man'd be a fool not to hold back enough to get home on. Not everybody pans out. It's a gamble."

Chuck changed the subject. "Were you planning on going along with Charles, Mrs. Flammarion?"

"Oh, no! This is *his* adventure."

"Wise decision," Doc said. "Hear tell some've done it. Hard place for a woman, especially"—he looked down at the table—"one as handsome as you, you don't mind me sayin' it."

"I don't fancy pulling a hundred-pound sled," I said, "or even leading a mule through ice and snow. I'll find a job in Skagway, and wait for . . . Charles to come back with his fortune."

"Skagway ain't no church picnic, neither," Doc said. "You might ought to stay in Seattle."

"I want to see him off. Make sure he's got a good mule and his shoes are tied."

"Mom . . ."

"But if Skagway is too rough, or I can't find a good job, I won't stay there. Go back to Juneau or Seattle."

"Not back home?"

I'd been telling the lie so long it almost felt true.

"Philadelphia, no. We left because there are too many sad memories there. My husband died recently."

"Oh." Doc and Chuck exchanged glances. "Then we have that in common, too. After my wife passed away, I couldn't bear living on the farm. So we sold it and decided to head for the Yukon."

"Neighbors said we were running away," Chuck said angrily.

"And if we were?"

"I'm sorry," I said. "Where was the farm?"

"Sedalia, Missouri." He gave me a wry smile. "It ain't Philadelphia. I took you for a city woman, Mrs. Flammarion." He pronounced it "*Flam*-reon."

"Call me Rosa," I said. "Everyone does."

"And I prefer Daniel," Daniel said. "Never did like Charles."

"Me neither," Chuck said.

"Saw you get on back there. You got kin in Kansas?"

Half a lie. "No, I took a temporary job teaching there. The school year's over, and when Daniel graduated, he decided he wanted to join the stampeders. I came along to see that he got a good start—and to see this part of the world."

"Yeah . . ." He looked out the window at the vague shapes sliding by in the darkness.

"Pop . . ." Chuck started.

"Uh-huh." He put his elbows on the table and looked straight at me. "Rosa, is your boy easy to get along with?"

"I generally find him so."

He shifted his gaze to Daniel. "Son, Chuck and me, we were just talkin' about takin' on a partner or two, at least as far as Dawson. Cost everybody less that way."

"Dad and me don't have ten years of school between us," Chuck said, "so you could help that way. But we know a heck of a lot about mules and shovels and all."

Daniel chewed his lower lip for a moment. He didn't look at me. "I would be glad to. Proud to." He smiled. "I don't know much about shovels."

Doc laughed. "Called 'em idiot sticks in the army. A stick with an idiot on one end and a shovel on the other."

I had a sudden cold feeling, but then realized Doc was only a few years older than me; he couldn't have been a Union soldier.

He saw my disquiet. "I wasn't much of a soldier. Spent two years in Texas lookin' for Indians; never found a one. Came back to farm and raise a family."

"You have other children?"

"Two daughters, both married. Two grandkids—had to get outa there, makin' me feel old."

We had to leave the dining car so others could have the table, but we moved into the lounge car for coffee and talked for a couple of hours about the world they were going to and the worlds we had left.

That was strange. The man and his son were direct, simple, honest folk, their life stories predictable and uncomplicated. Daniel and I had a life story that was a carefully woven fabric of lies, often rehearsed and elaborated on.

Doc's father had not served in the War Between the States, because of bad eyesight. Being half blind hadn't kept him from homesteading, though, and his small farm prospered and grew as his family grew. Except for his stint as an unsuccessful Indian fighter, the Missouri farm was almost all that Doc knew of the world. He had been to St. Louis a few times, and his experiences in that metropolis did not leave him looking forward to coping with San Francisco and Seattle. I promised to help them negotiate with merchants in putting together their "kits."

(Doc got his name by virtue of having taken a mail-order course of instruction in veterinary medicine. It was what we'd call a "degree mill" now, but I was to find out that he had a way with animals, and was intelligent, and knew his limits.)

We returned to our sleepers, but the coffee and excitement kept me awake for a long time. The last quarter moon rose into the clear night, and gave the snowy mountaintops an ethereal blue glow. I realized that hours had passed without my having thought about Edward or his Pinkerton men.

We had planned to get off the train as widely separated as possible, since the Pinkerton men would be looking for a young man in the company of his mother. It was possible they would have photographs.

I was thinking of how to explain this odd separation to the Colemans, and came to an obvious solution: we would get off with them, instead; a rustic family of four. I would let down my hair, and wear my plainest dress, with no corset. Daniel had jeans and a disreputable work shirt.

We played cards with them the next day, and chatted, as the train worked its way down the western slope of the Rockies, across a stretch of desert, and then through the riot of green that irrigation had brought to the California desert. Before we even got to Berkeley, Doc suggested we ought to get all our luggage in one place and try to stay together.

We had no idea what to expect. Wagons would transfer us and our baggage to a San Francisco ferry, where anything could happen. Assuming Daniel and I even made it off the platform.

The train squealed to a stop in a cloud of dust and smoke and steam, and if any of Edward's agents were looking for us, we gave them the slip. We put our things aboard a wagon and elected to walk alongside it.

It was a refreshing walk, July in Berkeley like May in Kansas. The streets were muddy ruts but there were boardwalks and, farther into town, sidewalks of brick and stone.

The ferry was crowded and slow, its steam engine hissing and clattering so loud we had to yell to converse.

The San Francisco dock was a crowded bedlam. Doc and I left the boys to stay with our things while we went to inquire about passage to Seattle.

An interesting thing happened while we were gone. There were lots of soldiers and sailors in the area. Daniel saw a Kansas flag and left Chuck to go talk to them.

They were headed for the Philippines, following the 20th Kansas, to which Daniel would have been attached in Topeka, had I signed for him to join underage. So he wouldn't have gone to follow the Rough Riders to glory in Cuba, after all. The Kansas troops were shipped overseas to, as the man who talked to Daniel put it, "go kill niggers in the Philippines."

Thank God Daniel hadn't gone with them. The truth of the Filipino insurrection was decades in coming, mainly because the truth was too horrible to accept: American soldiers killed at least 200,000—women and children as well as soldiers—and Kansas was at the front of the slaughter.

Pressed into my diary at this point is a later article from the *Anti-Imperialist League Journal*. Yellow and crumbling, it dropped into two pieces when I unfolded it. It quoted letters from the 20th Kansas: a captain said, "Caloocan was supposed to contain 70,000 inhabitants. The 20th Kansas swept through it, and now Caloocan contains not one living native." A private under him repeated that he himself had torched over fifty houses, killing women and children.

Twenty-two Kansans died there, out of more than a thousand in the regiment. Four deserted somehow. I wondered what Daniel could have done—what he could have become—faced with that scene of hellish extermination. And then six more months of slaughter.

Doc and I found a freighter willing to take us to Seattle for seven dollars apiece, though with absolutely no amenities. We were to come aboard immediately and wait until their holds were full and they could steam.

I stayed on the deck and guarded our things while the men went out for supplies. They came back with more beer and whiskey than I would have, but they also brought plenty of water and food and blankets, which would come in handy.

The men played whist while I wrote in my diary and read, and just before sundown the steamer's whistle screamed twice and she cast off. Once we were under weigh, it cooled off immediately, and clouds began to gather. We improvised a shelter in the last light, using one of the blankets as a sort of tent roof and cargo crates as walls. It began to rain, but we were dry and almost cozy, sitting around a candle, the men drinking whiskey while I made sandwiches and drank a whole beer. I even had a cup of water laced with whiskey, which tasted awful but warmed me inside.

After a while the first mate came down and bade

us put out the candle. I pointed out that it would be difficult to sustain a bonfire in this rain, and he admitted that was so, but he had regulations to enforce. So we surrendered to darkness and wrapped ourselves up in blankets, using bundles of clothing as pillows.

My diary makes no note of this, but I well remember that after the boys were sound asleep, Doc came to me, and we gave each other some comfort, stopping short of actual adultery.

The next morning he tried to talk me into coming along with them to the Yukon, and a part of me was tempted, but I demurred. This was Daniel's adventure, and having his mother along would spoil it for him.

("Adventure" is how I saw it; the physical challenge would be salutary, I thought, and I reluctantly admitted that it was time for the apron strings to be cut. Far better this than war.)

Seattle was even busier and more chaotic than San Francisco had been. None of the hotels near the water had any rooms vacant. Stampeders usually had to wait a week or more before finding passage north. After a long search, I found a room in a private home, a half mile from the outfitting stores on First and Second Avenues. The woman who rented it to me advised me to check with the Chamber of Commerce downtown, which maintained a Woman's Department for female prospectors. I didn't bother telling her that I was only going as far as Skagway.

I did have time to go by there before meeting the men at one thirty. It was interesting. They were basically set up to talk you out of going, but if you have to go, be prepared for this and that. They gave me a list similar to the one Doc and Chuck had, with a conspicuous addition: "a small revolver, to be carried on your person, with a quantity of appropriate ammunition."

The men were waiting for me in front of Nell's Chowder House, with the pushcart piled high with sacks of flour and beans and tins of bacon, coffee, tea, sugar, and so forth.

We had good chowder, keeping an eye on our things while exchanging stories about our morning's adventures. When I told them about the revolver, Doc got serious, and said he'd overridden his boy on that one, as well; they only carried a rifle, for game. Carrying a pistol would more likely get you into trouble than out of it, he said, echoing my sentiment.

Writing that down, I have to wonder again whether that was the turning point of all our lives. Everyone on this planet.

Doc and Chuck went off with an empty pushcart

and the list while I took Daniel and his heavily laden cart to our new home. I offered to help him push it up the hills, but he good-naturedly declined, saying there would be nothing *but* hills from Skagway on.

We unloaded the cart into our room and relaxed in the parlor for a while, having tea made with an electrical kettle. I realized it was one of the last times I would have alone with Daniel, and although I tried not to be sentimental, he sensed my natural anxiety and nervously tried to make light of the dangers he was facing.

He looked fit and strong. For years he had been working summers and weekends at the press room, and much of that was heavy lifting. He also lifted weights and wrestled at school, an enthusiasm that had left me both surprised and relieved.

We finished our tea and pushed the cart back down to the hurly-burly near the docks, where Doc and Chuck were waiting at the Chowder House. To our surprise and Daniel's delight, they had secured us space on a Russian steamer, the *White Nights*, leaving for Skagway the next day. Our accommodations were the same as we had enjoyed on the trip from San Francisco, a tent on the deck, but this time we had a real tent. And over a ton of food.

We examined the list and divided it in two, with

the Colemans basically going after hardware and Daniel and I gathering medicine, cooking utensils, and all the clothing except shoes and boots, which each would try on himself. We would also pick up the remaining food, evaporated milk and dried fruit, adding from my Chamber of Commerce list crystallized eggs, if we could find them, and lime juice to prevent scurvy—and improve the flavor of the cheap whiskey.

We would take our bounty directly to the ship, where there was supposed to be an armed guard for overnight security. Chuck volunteered to sleep with the goods, though, while the rest of us had one last night under a roof.

All three men were about the same size, so buying clothes was a simple matter of Dan trying them on and buying three sets. It was a bulky lot, rather than heavy, but we managed by lashing the pile down on the cart. Daniel couldn't see over the pile, so I had to guide him through the streaming crowd down to the docks and the *White Nights*. The gangway was steep and he did let me help pull the cart up.

The Colemans weren't there yet, and the officer on deck, a young man who seemed flustered by having a woman on board, spoke no English. He did respond to Daniel's Latin—the first time he had used it outside the classroom—and led us to our cache, an area marked off with red ribbons and COLMAN/FLE-MARION chalked on the deck.

We stacked the bags and boxes and then took a tour of the ship. "Rust bucket" was the term that Daniel used, and I just hoped it had enough sturdy rust to keep us afloat as far as Skagway. A lot of it was leaving the ship via a steady stream of brown water being pumped out from below.

The Russian ship had not been built with passengers in mind. It did have a large cargo area on deck, and that's what we were. The only concession to the cargo being human was an outhouse rigged over the stern.

We read and wrote until it began to get dark. I was starting to worry about the Colemans, when at last they heaved their way aboard, complaining that there wasn't a pick to be had in all of Seattle, though they did find four pick handles. I supposed they would be easy enough to come by in Skagway, though at an inflated price.

A Chinaman on the dock was selling fried fish and potatoes, so I sent Daniel down to get us some, while we settled accounts by candlelight. They asked me to do the addition and division, but I insisted we both do it, and compare results. After a couple of puzzling discrepancies were sorted out—Doc forgot to include the $120 he paid for the passage to Skagway—we came up with $1,833 divided three ways, with my giving the Colemans an extra fifty dollars for passage and my share of the food and drink going north. All told, we owed them $155, hardware being more expensive than clothing.

I gave Doc a five-dollar bill and six golden eagles. He gave three to his son and both laughed, hefting and clinking them, thinking about gold to come. We sealed the deal with whiskey, mine with a good portion of sugar-water and lime juice. Daniel arrived with the fish and we had an amiable dinner party. Then the three of us repaired up the hill, Doc and Daniel carrying sleeping bags, which elicited some drunken comments, that I pretended not to hear, from a man sitting on the curb. Doc excused himself and fell back to kick the man in both shins. I whispered thanks to him when he returned.

(I wasn't sure whether Daniel, with his back to us, was aware of either the insults or the retribution. I had never given him instruction in sexual matters, and it's possible he hadn't understood the man's innuendo.)

The landlady was reading in the parlor when we came in. She gave me a stern look, but said nothing but "Seventy-five cents if you want breakfast." We declined, saying we'd found a ship and would be leaving early.

I was a little nervous preparing for bed, lest Doc expect a repeat of the previous night's intimacy, which of course I couldn't do with Daniel in the room. But both men were asleep and snoring, exhausted, minutes after unrolling their sleeping bags. I suppose I was both relieved and annoyed.

We did have a hearty breakfast downtown, johnnycakes with bacon and eggs, which prompted Doc to go off in search of a couple of jugs of maple syrup. Daniel and I went on to the ship, so that Chuck could go ashore and eat before our ten thirty departure. Sitting on boxes, we played double solitaire and reminisced about Philadelphia and Dodge. As if by mutual agreement, his father's name never came up.

Doc returned triumphant from his hunt with two gallon jugs of syrup and, from the same place, several jars of various marmalades. He wouldn't take any payment for the addition to our stores. "Finally able to feed my sweet tooth," he said.

At ten, the first mate came around with his passenger list, checking us off like the items of cargo that we were. Then they got up a head of steam and cast off, five minutes early, and headed out into Puget Sound.

We were blessed with fine weather, and the boat's sway was not bothersome, at least to the human cargo. Some people had brought mules or horses, who weren't taking well to it.

Doc didn't hide his contempt for their owners, who had paid at least half the creatures' value for their passage. When they got to Skagway—if they survived—they would be weak and useless for days. Better to pay more at Skagway and get an animal that was proven and immediately useful.

Taking horses was a mistake, anyhow, Chuck said, and his father agreed. They cost less than mules, but it was a false economy, given the harsh environment in the Yukon. They were relatively delicate and stupid. In fact, two horses would die on the voyage, to be laboriously and unceremoniously winched overboard, while the mules became accustomed to shipboard life, placidly converting oats into a hygiene problem.

The scenery was beautiful along Puget Sound, fine woodland dominated by Mount Rainier. I sat and drew while the men joined a penny-ante poker game. (I thought of admonishing Daniel not to go in over his head, but kept silent.) The prospect of almost two weeks of doing nothing was pure balm after the past few days of frantic activity and worry.

We had left Edward behind for good. I looked at Daniel, with his scruffy beard and rough clothes—his ridiculous floppy sourdough hat—and realized his father wouldn't recognize him in a million years.

A modest proposal.

The steamer put in at Nunaimo as the sun was setting, to take on coal, and we were allowed a couple of
hours on shore. The boys took the first hour, and
came back merry from a pub.

Doc and I walked into town, enjoying the neat-
ness and quiet of it. Roses everywhere, their heavy
perfume a welcome respite from the barnyard smell
the deck had when the ship wasn't moving.

"Rosa, I have a matter to discuss with you," Doc
said, and from his evident nervousness I was pretty
sure what it was going to be. "I don't reckon you have

to say yes or no now, but you know, when we get back from the Yukon, I might could be pretty well set up, and a woman could do worse than me."

"A woman could do a lot worse than you right now, Doc." The future, about which I had avoided thinking, whirled through my mind in all its permutations, mostly dismal. I was tempted to tell him the simple truth—that in the eyes of the Lord I was still a married woman—and not give him false hope.

But we do live on hope, and he was headed for a burdensome time, and he was the protector of my child. A single thought struck me with electrical force, profound in its element of apostasy: *If God is just He will forgive me.*

"Let me think for a moment." We sat on a bench under a guttering gaslight and I took his hand in both of mine, a rash and forward gesture in that time.

"People change over time," I began.

"Not so much at our age, Rosa."

"True enough. You may be gone for years, though, and we've barely had a week to come to know each other. Let me only say this: that I pledge not to marry any other man until we meet again. Then we can see. Will that do?"

"More than I've got the right to ask." He took my hand and pressed it gently to his lips, a touching courtly gesture from a rough man. A man I "might could" grow to love.

We sat there holding hands for a few minutes, watching the lights of Vancouver coming on, across the bay. Then we wordlessly walked back down to the harbor, hand in hand.

There is some world, I'm sure, where Doc's vision of the future worked out. He made a fortune in the goldfields and came back to me; we married and were blessed with a late child, and lived happily ever after in Missouri. Not this world, though. This world I brought into existence by grieving.

When we got to the dock, he unrolled his pipe from its chamois wrap, and tamped precious tobacco into it, something he did only a few times a week. I remember the smells—leather and the sulfurous match, coal gas sputtering in the dock lights, the sweet briar aroma as he puffed it alight—I've never liked tobacco, but whenever I smell a pipe I think of Doc, even today, and of the worlds that are and were and might have been.

Plea for books and paper.

We slept well in the ship's slow roll, lulled by the monotonous throb of the engine, and in the morning I made the same breakfast that would sustain us most mornings until Skagway—bacon and eggs and pancakes. We had a patent "Yukon stove," safe to use on board. It had a hand-cranked fan to get the fuel alight—newspaper and a few lumps of coal, in our case.

We moved through vistas of great beauty, the snowcapped Cascade Range to our right—though I had awakened to what I at first thought had been an unsettling dream, the boat hurtling out of control down an absurdly narrow cataract. In fact, it was half true; we had gone through the Seymore Narrows, all that water squeezed through a passage only a few hundred yards wide. By noon we had an unpleasant situation of an opposite nature—we moved into the open sea, Queen Charlotte Sound, and for several hours the ship was tossed around like a toy boat. Our kit was secure, but that wasn't true of everybody's. There was a fury of chasing around cans that rolled all over the deck, and inevitable disputes over ownership.

One such dispute came to blows, and then the men circled each other with knives on the pitching deck, with an audience about equally divided between those wanting to stop it and those eager for blood. Eventually, the first mate fired a pistol into the air and declared in broken English that if one of them was cut the other one would die. With an exchange of profane language, the men retreated to their respective sides.

Doc predicted the two would be friends again tomorrow—that they had just worked themselves into a situation where neither could back down without being humiliated in public. He was right; the next day I saw them chatting amiably together.

By evening we were back in protected waters, and there were no more dramatic disputes during the three days we churned north to Fort Wrangell. I was amused to find that none of my three men had the slightest idea about how to make bread, though they were carrying over a thousand pounds of flour! They were going to live on flapjacks and hard biscuits. I taught them the rudiments, and by Wrangell each one of them could use the Yukon stove, with its baking enclosure, to make a thing that at least resembled a loaf of bread, though some of it was so dense it might serve better as a weapon than as food.

Fort Wrangell was surprising, to put it mildly. My five-year-old Baedeker said it was "a dirty and dilapidated settlement inhabited by about 250 Tlingits and a few whites." Instead we came upon a town that from the water appeared bigger and more prosperous than Dodge.

(And indeed it had a connection to Dodge: Wyatt Earp had been marshal of both towns. The paper I bought on the dock noted that he had quit the post and gone north ten days after being sworn in. "Wrangell was too tough for him," it said, but I supposed he was just marking time before heading for the gold.)

We had to wait at anchor for a place at the dock,

as there were two other steamers loading and unloading. One was taking on lumber; the fresh smell of pine wafted over the water. When the wind shifted, there were less pleasant smells from a fish cannery and a brewery.

When we did dock, the first mate announced that we were staying overnight, leaving at first light. The Wrangell Narrows are difficult to negotiate even during the day; we didn't want to be stuck in them after sundown. That was fine with us, after four days confined to the deck of the ship.

The boys hurried off while Doc and I strolled down the main street—Front Street, which was really just an extended dock, boards spiked onto pilings. There was a temporary feel to it, and there weren't nearly as many people around as the size of the place would justify. Doc eventually sorted it out in a conversation with a publican: A few months before, there might have been a thousand or more prospectors, headed up the Stikine River for the Teslin Trail to the Klondike. But that trail was rough and long, and now that the Chilkoot Pass was open, everybody went on to Skagway and Dyea. That was why none of the flyers or posters we'd seen had mentioned Fort Wrangell.

We got to the end of Front Street and I saw a sign

pointing toward the Mission School for Girls, and gave Doc leave to go back to a tavern he had eyed longingly. It was Saturday, so the school would probably be deserted, but I was curious. Doc protested that we'd seen some rough-looking men on the street. I opened my purse and showed him the Pinkerton man's revolver.

I didn't see any men, rough-looking or otherwise, on the ten-minute walk to the school. It was a peeled-log structure with a tarpaper roof, and had seen better days.

There was no sound inside, but when I pushed on the door, it creaked open. "Hello?" a woman's voice said.

It took my eyes a moment to adapt to the darkness within; the few windows were small and cloudy. A slight, gray-haired woman was seated at a desk opposite the door.

"Sorry—I didn't mean to intrude. . . ."

"Oh, please do intrude. I'm grading tests."

I walked over and took her hand and introduced myself. She was Grace Loden. I told her we had something in common: I'd been teaching Sunday school to Arapaho Indians in Dodge City.

"Mine are less fierce," she said. "The Tlingits haven't scalped anybody in almost fifty years. And those were Russians." She stood up. "Let's go outside. I've been sitting here for hours."

We compared notes. The Tlingit, despite their sometimes fierce appearance, aren't especially warlike, and although they weren't easy to convert, they did seem interested in Christianity, and were glad to have her teaching their daughters. The sons were another matter; they were taught by the island's elders and shamans.

Grace seemed about my age but looked older, her face seamed with lines of fatigue and worry. Her carriage was stooped. We went to a log propped on two boulders and sat.

She gestured at one of the monuments. "You know the expression 'low man on the totem pole'? That's me. The church that sponsors the school is in Sitka, four hundred miles away. They have their own concerns, including their own school. They do get some education money from the Territory, but it's sporadic and unpredictable. And even once I have some money, I can't just walk down the street and buy books and pencils and paper.

"Sometimes we peel bark off the beech trees and write on it with ink made from berry juice. The children enjoy that but it's distracting and makes a mess."

I told her that we'd be stopping at Sitka for several

hours, and asked whether I could deliver a message from her. It's easy to file a letter away, but a person standing in front of you has to be dealt with.

She was effusively grateful. We went back to the mission school, and she lit an old-fashioned oil lamp, just a rush sitting in oil, and took it to her desk. It gave off a greasy, disagreeable odor, reinforcing the general smell of the place.

"Seal oil," she said as she sat down at her desk and took out a sheet of paper. "Sit anywhere, Rosa. This will only take a minute."

About forty small desks were grouped in three sections, clustered around a central potbellied stove. A chalkboard behind the teacher's desk, and another on the opposite wall.

There were charts with the alphabet and times tables, and, oddly out of place, a periodic table of the elements. Maps of Alaska and the world. Some student drawings pinned up, most of them crude, but a couple at one end, ink renderings of totem poles, showed a lot of care and skill. Their complex shapes would be hard to draw; I'd thought about doing that when we docked, but decided they would take too long.

She sanded the letter and addressed an envelope while it was drying. We stepped out into the cool fresh air and she handed both to me. "Try to see Reverend Bower first. He actually controls the purse strings. If he's not in, Mrs. Archer will do—you might want to talk to her anyhow, teacher to teacher."

The letter was an urgent request for secondary readers in history and religion, which could be hand-me-downs from the Sitka school, along with a standing order for pen points, ink, and loose paper of any description, preferably lined. She closed with a note of urgency: *September is closer than it seems; my secondary students need the novelty of new materials, or they may stop coming. Their parents won't force them.*

I folded the letter carefully and put it in the envelope. I checked my watch and asked whether she would like to break bread with us aboard ship. She accepted avidly.

The men were still out wandering through the town and woods. I fired up the stove and made us generous sandwiches of bacon and onion, with English mustard. The bread was Chuck's latest attempt, not too stonelike. We had mugs of cool cider that had just begun to turn. While we were eating I started some bacon for the men and gave Grace an abbreviated version of our collective story.

"Be careful in Skagway," she said. "The town is run by a committee of thieves and rogues led by a man called Soapy Smith. There isn't any real law other than what he wants to happen."

"We should be able to stay out of his way," I said. "There must be thousands of people there."

She nodded. "Maybe fifteen thousand, this time of year. Eager to get over the pass before the first snow. Your timing is pretty good—though if you want to make some money, rather than going through the slow torture of carrying all this stuff to the Yukon, I'd put it up for sale on the dock in Skagway! You'd probably get twice what you paid for most of it, and get back to Seattle before you see a flake of snow."

I laughed at that. "I'll suggest it. Somehow I doubt that my boys will have much enthusiasm."

I was starting to worry about them. Some of the passengers and crew were coming back, and though the crew were jabbering in Russian, it was pretty obvious that we hadn't stopped here just for the water. A cluster of girls apparently no older than Daniel stood on the dock and waved at them, giggling.

She followed my glance. "Your boy is . . . not experienced?"

"I don't think so. I'm almost certain not. Likewise Chuck, if my instincts are at all good."

"We have several girls a year made pregnant by sailors and tourists," she said. "They have to go someplace else. It's sad. Some of them wind up in Seattle or San Francisco, with only one way to make a living. Or even worse." She paused, looking at the girls waving. "Or better . . . the shamans have ways to stop the pregnancy."

"Murder the unborn child?" Of course I knew about that in "civilized" society.

"They don't see it that way," she said, her face set in a way that reinforced the downward lines.

Chuck and Doc came up the gangway carrying a basket and a fish, a large salmon. They'd been shopping. "Fresh caught," Doc said. "It only cost a quarter."

"Smoked venison," Chuck said, "a penny a strip."

"But it won't keep," I said to Doc.

"Won't have to. I'll cut us off four steaks and shop the rest around. Guarantee I'll get more than the quarter back."

Daniel came aboard with a strange unreadable look on his face. Oh no, I thought. But he had one hand behind his back and held it out to me.

It was beautiful. On a leather thong, a cross carved from ivory, with a circle in its center, elaborated with complex intaglio. Red jewels were set where Jesus' hands and feet had been.

"It's Russian style," he said. "It might be old."

I put it around my neck and kissed him. To my surprise, he kissed me back. "We won't be together, Christmas," he said in a hoarse whisper.

I found my voice and introduced Grace. They all talked while I busied myself making sandwiches. Cutting the onions brought tears.

A horrible accident.

In the morning we could appreciate the sailors' concern over the Wrangell Narrows. We had to negotiate a slow winding course marked off by buoys and stakes, sometimes with only a couple of yards' leeway.

Most ships would steam straight up to Juneau, but the *White Nights* had cargo bound for Sitka, the territorial capital and the only large place in Alaska with a Russian population. The ship was carrying books and magazines in that language, and cases of vodka, which at that time was not well known in the United States.

So we turned west and then backtracked south for a day. The prospectors grumbled about it, but of course I didn't mind—a few more days with my son, and an exotic small city to visit.

We were about twenty miles from Sitka when disaster struck. There was an explosion belowdecks, followed by an unearthly noise: the shriek of steam escaping, combined with a man's dying wail.

They brought him up on the deck. I hope never to see a more horrible sight. The flesh from one side of his face had been flayed off completely, nothing but glistening grayish bone and the ruin of an eye. His throat and shoulder on that side were just a mass of gore, and most of his upper body was as red as a lobster. As they laid him down on the deck, he took a few bubbling breaths and was still. The anchor chain rattled down.

The prospectors and sailors stood around his body in a silent circle. Then one of the crew came to his side and fell to both knees, put his hands together, and said what must have been a prayer in Russian, ending in a sob.

Two men went below and returned with a coffin. It was sobering to note that they were prepared for death that way. I wondered how many such boxes they carried.

The first mate issued a few quiet orders, and most of the crew went off to lower a boat. It drifted away from us with three aboard, who raised a simple lateen sail and then moved swiftly downstream.

Leon, the crew member who was easiest with English, explained the situation to us. It was plain luck, he said, that many more were not injured or killed. The boiler's emergency valve apparently got clogged— it was like a pressure-cooker plug of soft metal—and before anybody saw what was happening, a seam burst. The dead man, Pyotr, had been the only person on that side of the boiler.

The men in the boat were going to Sitka to arrange for a tow. There was no way they could repair the boiler with the tools on board. We would be in Sitka for as long as it took us to repair or replace the boiler.

The prospectors accepted this with uncharacteristic silence, after the sudden confrontation with mortality.

The crew took the coffin below, and the mood became less morbid. I remained deeply shaken, and Daniel was pallid. When the men started loud talk and laughter, I wanted to shush them—but of course they were only dealing with it in their own way. There was a lot of whiskey going around, and some of the crew came up on deck with a ceramic jug of vodka, which they poured into small glasses, to drink in single gulps. The prospectors traded with them, and pronounced it firewater, I believe as a compliment. The Russians said no; water of life. A young man offered me a glass, but I declined.

(If it had been wine, I would have taken it gladly, for its calmative effect—but my recent experience with whiskey had taught me to expect the opposite from spirits.)

I had never felt so conspicuous, for being the only woman on board. Some of the men might have expected me to faint or weep at the horrible sight—or at least go to the rail and vomit, as many of them had—but I've never thought the "weaker" sex was actually weaker in that regard. From childbirth, I knew more about pain and gore than most of them. From three miscarriages, I knew enough about horror. Seeing a stranger die was nothing compared to having life within you die, and expelling the remains.

(Our house in Philadelphia had had a fainting couch, which I would sometimes resort to when I couldn't stand Edward's company. It probably made him smug in his masculine superiority.)

It was still light around nine, when the rescue tug clattered up the strait. She came alongside and threw a couple of light lines over, tied to thick hawsers. The crew hauled in the hawsers and made them fast to cleats, while others were cranking up the anchor, shouting directions and orders around in Russian. Without being able to understand a word, you could hear the impatience, the need for haste. There wouldn't be any moon, I knew, so it would be pitch dark for a few hours around midnight, and the captain probably didn't want to be stranded by dark, the way we'd been in Wrangell.

We made good time, though, and the channel markers as we approached Sitka had bobbing lamps. The first mate announced that we would be in port at least two days; if anybody wanted to take a room ashore, a crew member would be keeping watch over our kits.

That sounded good to all four of us, and we were the first down the gangplank. There was a boy waiting there who asked whether we wanted rooms, and led us two blocks to the Baranoff Hotel, an unprepossessing two-story shack with whitewash that had gone gray.

Inside, the smell of fresh coffee, and an old woman whose chirpy alertness made me feel like a heavy sleepwalker. Her rooms were nine dollars a night, meals included. That seemed high—a month's rent in Dodge—but none of us had the spirit to argue over it.

Daniel was still sleeping soundly after I'd arisen and had breakfast—as were Chuck and Doc, and for the same reason; I sincerely hoped their whiskey wouldn't run out before they got to Skagway. I left Daniel a note and got directions to the Sheldon Jackson Industrial College, to deliver Grace's plea for books and supplies.

The morning was bright and cool, the salt breeze refreshing. Plenty of people and traffic for such a small place—but at that time Sitka was still the territorial capital, as well as Alaska's oldest city. The Russian influence remained here and there. A church bell rang the hour, eight o'clock, and when I glanced up the hill at the sound, I saw it was an Eastern Orthodox church, the one where the crewman would be buried today.

The Sheldon Jackson School wasn't hard to find, the only octagonal building made of concrete in Sitka, or Alaska, or possibly North America. In the foyer there was a chalkboard with names and room numbers.

Halfway around the octagon I found the door to Benjamin Bower's office open. He was a large florid man with a neatly trimmed salt-and-pepper beard. He was jacketless, wearing a plaid weskit with a heavy golden watch chain. Busy watering flowers at the window, he made a startled little jump when I tapped on the door.

"Reverend Bower?"

"Come in, come in." He turned his attention back to the watering. "Fast work. Commendable."

"Pardon me?"

"You're the first. The notice only went out yesterday noon." He looked up. "You *are* a teacher."

"In fact, I am. But I'm not here about a notice."

"Ah. Hum." He set down the watering can and looked over my shoulder, lost in thought for a moment. "Have a seat, please, Miss, Mrs. . . ."

I smelled a job but made a quick decision. "Flammarion—Rosa Flammarion."

"Ah. Very good." He eased himself down into a chair and pulled it up to his desk, wheels squeaking. "And what can I do for a Southern lady this far north?" For some men I use a little more Georgia than for others.

"I've just come from Fort Wrangell." I took the envelope out of my purse. "Grace Loden asked me to bring this to you."

He sighed. "Let me show you a demonstration of

mentalism, Mrs. Flammarion." He touched the corner of the envelope to his temple and squeezed his eyes shut. "She needs money."

"Not so much money as books and supplies," I said. "She's in a really bad way. Old books, anything."

He nodded and slowly slit the letter with a jade opener. He kept nodding as he read it. "Old textbooks might be possible. There's little money. You don't have religious contract schools down south, do you?"

"I taught in Kansas. We once had them—I taught in a secular school, but gave religious instructions to the Indians in an old Presbyterian one-room schoolhouse."

He raised an eyebrow at that. "We used to be a Presbyterian contract school. We could count on about forty, even sixty percent of our expenses to be covered by the church—until a couple of years ago."

I'd heard something of that. "The government?"

"That's right. They closed down the system, on constitutional grounds, supposedly—and *supposedly* the federal government would make up the loss. But we're not a state. So we're the small pig at the trough, if you'll excuse a barnyard metaphor." He rolled his chair to a low bookshelf under the window and selected the last in a series of worn ledgers. He rolled back, his nimbleness almost comical, set the ledger next to Grace's letter, and flipped through it.

"I think—here." He put his finger on an entry. "I *can* help her on the McGuffey readers. We got fifty new ones back in April; the old ones would be in the library back room. I'll have them boxed up. You're on the steamer that had the . . . unfortunate accident?"

"Yes, the *White Nights*."

He nodded and put his glasses back in their case with a snap. "It will call at Fort Wrangell on the way back. Miss Loden will have her books. And I can find her some composition books and pencils. Could you make sure that they get to her?"

"I won't be aboard. We're getting off at Skagway."

"Skagway?" He tilted his head at me. "You're not going prospecting."

"No; my son is, and a couple of friends. I want to see them off safely."

"See to your own safety, too. It's a coarse and dangerous place."

"I know. Miss Loden told me to watch out for Soapy Smith and his gang."

He laughed. "Unless I've misread your character, I don't think you'll ever see Soapy Smith. He's in a much hotter place than Alaska now."

I was a little slow. "Hotter?"

"Mr. Smith died in a gunfight last week. There was some sort of a town meeting about him, on the wharf, to which he wasn't invited. When he tried to force his way in, a guard shot him. He killed the guard as well, as his dying act."

"God rest their souls."

He pursed his lips and nodded. "Skagway should be noticeably calmer when you and your boy get there. What then? Back to Kansas?"

"No. I've had enough of that. I thought I'd try my luck in Seattle or San Francisco."

"Teaching what grades?"

"I did nine through twelve in Kansas."

"There's a job here, tailor made for you, teaching and missionary work. Not much competition."

"I don't know that I could—"

"You'd be close to your son, Mrs. Flammarion. And to us you'd be a godsend." He shrugged and smiled. "God's will, perhaps."

I tried to read his character as he had mine. "Mr. Bower, may I entrust you with a secret?"

He smiled. "If it doesn't involve a hanging offense."

"I left a bad marriage. I can't go back to Kansas because he found me there."

"You don't believe in divorce?"

"No I do not."

"Let me hazard a guess: you are not actually related to a French astronomer and novelist."

"That's correct. I can't use my real name; that's how he found me, after four years. My son tried to join the army."

He rubbed his beard and stared at the desktop for a long moment. "You don't want to talk about why you left him."

"No. Except to assure you that it was the only course. For my only child's safety."

"I do believe you." He closed the ledger quietly. "You know . . . Alaska has a fairly difficult examination for teachers. One's performance on that means more than, say, academic records. You've been to college."

"Wellesley."

"Boston. You might find our winters no worse here." He anticipated my question. "I don't suppose we'd have to bother them about a transcript if you did well on the test."

"Well, then. I should like to arrange to take it."

He reached into a bottom drawer and brought out a large white envelope. "Do you have a pencil?"

I was given three hours and an empty classroom. At ten o'clock, children filled the hall, laughing and screaming. It was only a little distracting, and soon enough they were properly caged up. Reverend Bower had warned me about that—regular school wasn't in session, but there was instruction in crafts, music, and dance.

The science and mathematics parts of the test were easy, stopping short of calculus. English was also simple, sentence diagramming and rules of grammar. Some of the history was difficult—for some reason, there were no questions about the history of Kansas, and I had never taught the history of Alaska! If they could make allowances for that, I was pretty confident.

I took the test back to Reverend Bower. He sealed it and signed across the flap, with time and date. "You had another forty-five minutes. The test was not too hard?"

"Except for Alaskan history, no. I could study that and retake it."

"Yes, of course." He scribbled something under his signature. "The territorial board meets tomorrow, down at city hall. I should have word in the afternoon, if your steamer is still here. Could you come by about three or four?"

Of course I would; I asked him to send word on to Skagway if I had to go on. He said he'd try but wasn't sanguine. School wouldn't start until Monday, September 5th, though; I could be back in plenty of time to find out about the job and, if I were accepted, prepare for classes.

It was still a beautiful morning, and rather than go back to the rooming house, I explored the town a bit. It had a much more permanent feel than Fort Wrangell; it had been the Russian base of operations before Seward's Folly. Some of their substantial log buildings were still in use, almost a century old.

I stopped in the office of the weekly paper, the *Alaskan,* and bought a copy. Reverend Bower's advertisement for a high school teacher was prominent, on the last page. The other jobs listed for women were menial and low-paying. (There was an article about communicable diseases sweeping San Francisco, with troops coming from all over to muster for the Philippines—it's just as well we had gone quickly in and out.)

The man at the newspaper office directed me to the Presbyterian mission, over on the Tlingit side of town. There used to be a stockade fence separating the two areas; the only thing left of it was a dilapidated watchtower. I guessed the lumber had long since been scavenged for building or fuel.

There's a museum full of Tlingit crafts and lore on

the mission grounds. I gave it a cursory look, planning to return, and followed a sign to the Indian River Walk. That was a couple of miles of pathway along a charming brook; just what I needed, except for the mosquitoes, large and aggressive. Absent the snow-topped mountains, I could have been back in the rural Massachusetts I loved as a college student.

Coming back into town, I saw Daniel and the Colemans fishing with hand lines off the dock. I thought that was typically male—what would they do if they caught one, eat it raw?—but in fact the lady at the rooming house had loaned them the equipment and said she would cook up their catch. So far they hadn't had any luck, but it was pleasant to sit with them and have an iced root beer out of their bucket.

They'd checked the situation at the *White Nights,* and although no one there could speak English, they could see that the boiler was disassembled, so we wouldn't be leaving right away. That was good news for me, of course; I told them about the morning's interview and test. Daniel's reaction was subdued; he thought I shouldn't commit to anything here until I'd checked Skagway. I had to laugh at that, and I'm afraid I embarrassed him, saying if they didn't need teachers, I could always get a job as a dance-hall girl or barmaid. You'd make ten times as much money, Doc said, which was probably true.

There was a faint regular knocking sound, coming from the *White Nights*: a muffled drum. The cabin boy marched down the gangway with the drum, followed by six men struggling with the coffin on their shoulders, and then the crew, dressed in a motley way, some in the work clothes they wore on deck and some in coat and tie. From fifty yards away, we could smell mothballs and the tang of celluloid collars.

The first mate, in what I suppose was a Russian naval uniform, saw us, and with an inclination of his head invited us to join the procession. I was torn between curiosity and an instinct not to intrude, but the men shrugged, tied their lines to pilings, and trotted down the dock, so I went along, too.

There was a Russian priest waiting at the graveyard behind the church. He wore red, and my memory of the scene is like an overexposed Kodachrome, his scarlet against the verdant green and the cloudless hard blue sky. At his feet, the dark scattered earth and deep hole.

He surprised us by speaking in unaccented English, about this man's long journey through life, and the short one he was now to undertake; about the mystery of God's will and our need to accept it without question. Then he spoke in faltering Russian, the captain whispering words when he paused.

His Russian was more sure when he slipped into memorized liturgy. He sang a hymn in a deep rich voice, the ship's crew mumbling along, the way their American counterparts would. Then they removed the boards supporting the coffin and lowered it with ropes. The priest threw a handful of dirt after it and said a few words. The captain and his men repeated the gesture; the first mate said softly to me, "You, please, too." Well, we had shared part of his journey. The soil was surprisingly warm and dry.

Reading that fifty-year-old diary, I wondered what would have happened if he hadn't died there. The worlds I gained for his losing this one.

Signs and portents.

There was a great amount of clatter and the ring of hammers on metal that afternoon, and then they fired up the boiler; most of the men up on the deck or, like us, standing on the dock alongside. Then the whistle blasted two short notes and two long, our signal, and repeated it twice. The first mate shouted down that we wouldn't depart until first light, and so could have another night on shore if we wished. Momentarily torn between parsimony and comfort, all four of us opted for feather beds.

The next morning I sat in the stern and watched

Sitka recede as we made our way up the Chatham Strait toward Juneau. It was a strange feeling. I would be back in a week or two, a completely different woman. Childless for the first time since my twenties.

I was not too concerned about whether I would be accepted for the job. I could survive for more than a year on the money I had, and if Sitka didn't have anything for me, there were certainly jobs in Seattle and San Francisco, and (I thought until the next day) even Juneau, which was larger than Sitka, two years away from being named the new capital.

We saw icebergs for the first time as we steamed past the Icy Strait. An otherworldly blue, pieces of them as small as carriages bobbed past us—though they were actually eight times as large, most of their bulk underwater. (We found out the crew hoped there would be plenty of southbound cargo in Juneau and Skagway; otherwise they'd be filling the hold with ice bound for San Francisco, arduous, freezing work.)

That night we endured the first heavy rain since Fort Wrangell. The ship slowed almost to a stop in the poor visibility. We huddled around candles, wrapped in damp blankets, while I read Edgar Allan Poe stories to them, for a different kind of chill.

A strange thing happened while I was reading Poe—doubly strange for me—an actual raven appeared, landing on the deck with a clatter and caw. Odd to see a bird out in that storm, and weird that it should be a raven.

Daniel had read the poem, and he looked pale. "If that thing says 'nevermore,' I'm going to jump over the side." He started to explain that to Doc and Chuck.

I knew what it was going to say, though.

It hopped to within a yard of me, cocking its head. It was close enough that I could see the glint of candle in its eye. "No gold," it said.

"'No go'?" Doc said.

It took a hop toward him. "No *gold!*" Doc aimed a kick at it, and it barely got out of the way. Another kick and it flew off into the wind.

"Jesus." Doc shook his head. "Signs and portents."

"Mom used to say that," Chuck explained.

"Maybe that's enough reading for tonight," I said.

"Aye." Doc blew out the candle and patted my hand in the darkness.

I couldn't sleep for a long time, haunted by a sense of prophecy. The raven's "no gold" had saved us twice, and the meaning now was just as clear. I wished I had told them about the other times. It would sound false now.

The boys also tossed and turned until the storm

abated and a thin gray light showed the fast-scudding clouds.

We could hear Juneau a long time before we saw it, though the incessant banging noise was not from the city proper, but rather from the rock-crushing factory across the bay. Dockside, the noise was as loud as a carpenter would be, hammering in the next room without letup.

How could they stand it? We rolled up wads of paper to block our ears, to little effect. The crew loaded and unloaded in a fast, nervous way; they wanted to get out before dark.

A calm man in a business suit came aboard, a local merchant checking the storage of his furs. When I asked him whether the noise ever let up, he said, "No, not even on Christmas. After awhile, you don't hear it anymore." I said it would drive me insane before I could get used to it.

"Maybe that's our secret," he said with a wink. "You have to be mad to stay here. But it's the sound of money. You don't hear that much in the States nowadays."

They said we would be here for three or four hours, at least, so I asked Doc whether he would accompany me in search of a cup of coffee, while the boys went off to a saloon. He readily agreed. I could have gone alone, but I didn't see any other un-escorted women on the "street," which was actually a steep river of mud. A lot of the men wore pistols, swaggering along, which I hadn't seen in Sitka. Doc said it was probably because people carried "pokes" of gold here. That made my poke of double eagles feel more heavy than usual.

About halfway up the hill we found a café with a card in the window advertising an Edison Spring Motor Phonograph on the premises. When we walked in, the proprietor started a cylinder of Scott Joplin, melancholy and merry at the same time, not quite loud enough to drown out the hammering across the bay.

The man was friendly but strange-looking, immensely fat and both hairless and toothless. He brought us a plate of pastries he said his wife had baked. Rich and delectable, they partly explained his size, and perhaps his lack of teeth.

This was the first time either of us had heard one of the "brown wax" cylinders, much more clear than their predecessors. We were fascinated, even though the cylinders were only good for two minutes of music, and he only had a dozen of them.

Between Doc's beer and my coffee, we were for some reason compelled to talk about our pasts—I stuck to the part that was true, childhood to courting. He was feeling sentimental, I think aided by the music, and recalled his wife, Lilian, with a candor that would have been embarrassing if it had been any other man talking. With Doc it was natural and endearing. Their love had been intense and physical, and he had no command of polite words for describing it—so he used barnyard terms in a reverent private whisper.

Strange how things turn out. We would be here again, and all the world would change. But this time we were a day or two away from parting, perhaps forever. I realize now that Doc's outpouring was driven by a premonition of death. He had never told anybody about his love and his loss in such detail. Describing it to me was a way of keeping his love alive.

Reading over these words, I can see that it sounds as if Doc were obliquely trying to seduce me. I don't think so at all; we had an unspoken understanding about that. The fact that we had known one another intimately did give him leave to talk plainly, and he was aching to talk, to memorialize Lilian.

Fifty years later, I think I have every record Scott Joplin ever made. When I put them on it's as close to a time machine as most people will ever experience.

Cleanliness and godliness.

We were ten miles upriver by the time the noise faded. One day out of Skagway, and the excitement on deck was palpable.

The crowd of prospectors became more sociable, walking around discussing plans and comparing kits. One fellow noticed that we had an overabundance of rifle ammunition, twelve bandoliers of sixty rounds each, and he offered to buy a couple of them. Doc took a sample bandolier around the deck and wound up selling half of them for ten times what he had paid, hiding his glee behind a serious expression. (They hadn't been a totally honest purchase in the first place, coming from an army sergeant who had certainly misappropriated them.)

Pretty soon, "horse trading" was the order of the day. Everyone knew how expensive things were reported to be in Skagway, so they compared their own kit to the ones around them. "You don't got near enough bacon," one would say; "how 'bout I trade you two tins and two dollars for that extra axe?"

We were approached by several entrepreneurs who noted that our kit was too small for four people— evidence of how little communication there had been on deck. After it became common knowledge that I was going back after Skagway, some of them diffidently asked if I might post a letter or two. Skagway had a bad reputation for mail delivery. You could wait in line all day, only to have the service window close in your face.

Two men had procured a guitar and fiddle in Juneau. The fiddler could carry a tune, but the guitarist had never played before, and was attempting to learn from a booklet that came with the instrument. Before long, there was a spirited bidding for the guitar, to be used as fuel—though the coalition that won the auction, at twelve dollars, simply smashed it to pieces and threw it over the rail, to tumultuous applause. Even the owner of the guitar laughed—and suddenly I realized that it must have been set up in advance! The *soi-disant* musician was as loud and annoying as he could be, and his accomplice started the bidding, to drop out when it got sufficiently high.

The water was very calm, and passage swift, and when the sun went down a party atmosphere prevailed, the fiddler joined by a boy with a harmonica and some improvised drumming. Men danced with energy, alone and together. Several asked me, but I had to demur out of ignorance. I would have gotten the rod for dancing as a child, and the ballroom dancing I learned at Wellesley was a little too stately for these reels and jigs.

But then Doc shyly offered to waltz with me, and I had to say yes. The music was not three-four time, and he danced like a stork, but it was good to be in his arms. We ignored the initial hooting and it dwindled away.

I had a strange premonitory feeling: suppose I said yes, Doc, I will marry you, but only if you give this up and come back to the States, to start up a normal life. Would Daniel and Chuck give up the Yukon?— surely not. And I wanted Doc, with his steadiness and knowledge, to be there with my boy.

When I woke at dawn (chastely apart from Doc) we were maneuvering into the one space available at Skagway's crowded wharf. We'd heard about the wharf and what a difference it made for new arrivals: had we come a year earlier, the steamer would have anchored out in deep water, while our goods were laboriously transferred by small boats to the mud at the high-tide mark. Horses and mules would have to swim ashore. Women and children were carried over the last hundred yards of mud—if they had someone willing to carry them.

In contrast, this wharf was a paragon of comfort and modernity—there were even electric lights, snapping off as the dawn brightened.

I had envisioned a place that was mostly tents and mud, with a few hastily constructed saloons, but there actually was a substantial town past the wharf, bigger than Fort Wrangell, even though most of the buildings couldn't have been more than a year old. I caught the smell of fresh pine just as the characteristic whine of a sawmill started up.

There were scores of people waiting on the dock, some with wagons for hire to transport your kit out to the tent town. Doc told the boys to stay put while he went down to see whether that was a luxury we could afford. I went along with him, both hesitant and curious.

Right at the bottom of the gangway was a little gray-haired lady with a stack of newspapers, the Skagway *News.* I found a dime and bought one, and told her I was surprised and relieved to see a woman at work here alone.

"Plenty of trouble for women here," she said with a twinkle in her eye, "especially for them as wants it." She introduced herself as Barbara, from Butte, Montana. I later found out that she was a local "character," saving her pennies while she lived inside a piano box that she'd bought for two dollars.

Most of the other women who came down to the ship were obviously women of easy, or no, virtue, but they weren't offensive in their behavior. They just stood around trying to look attractive, which frankly was a task beyond most of their powers.

Doc asked all of the men with wagons, and the cheapest one he could find was fifteen dollars. We had a powwow about that, and decided it would be worth it if the driver would promise not to unload our goods until we agreed on a proper site. He said that wouldn't be a problem; there were dozens of places pretty close to town.

The deck was a madhouse of activity, mostly heavy lifting and cussing, so I let the men take care of both aspects. I went down to the end of the dock and got them a pail of coffee, but otherwise just stayed out of the way, reading the paper.

The storm we had weathered on the way into Juneau had been severe enough to make the news. We were lucky to have been inland; a river steamer like ours, the *Mable Lane*, had sunk in the Bering Sea.

There was a story about the funeral for Frank Reid, the man who had killed Soapy Smith on the 8th of July. The two men had evidently fired simultaneously, Reid suffering a shattered spine. He lingered in agony for twelve days, the church choir singing in an attempt to alleviate his misery and "bring him back to God." What a hard way to go.

By the time I finished the short paper, the men had the wagon nearly loaded. They swung aboard with the kit while I hoisted myself up to sit uncomfortably close to the wagoneer. He smelled worse than any of the men on the boat, none of them paragons of hygiene. His face and exposed forearms were crusty with open sores, and all his teeth were rotten. I would rather have walked alongside in the mud, but we were off as soon as I was settled.

I *could* have walked in a third of the time, too, as

the tent town was waking up and the mud road was crowded with people and animals. The wagoneer kept up a constant stream of muttered oaths that exploded into shouted imprecations when necessary.

He did find us a place, though; a recently vacated square of almost dry dirt. Doc paid him and he amiably helped the men unload. The things that were not too heavy for me to lift, I unloaded and stacked along one edge of our temporary homestead.

We had gotten a sheet of printed instructions along with the tent, but they were nowhere to be seen. The boys tried to improvise its erection while Doc and I searched for the directions. We found the sheet eventually, safely hidden inside a box of dry goods, by which time the boys had strung together a misshapen skein of rope and canvas. Several neighbors watched with interest.

The neighbors did help, though, once we had the canvas and poles laid out according to the diagram. It was good to have several men pulling on the ropes. By the time we were finished, the canvas was tight as a drumhead.

One neighbor sold me a bale and a half of straw for a dollar, and I floored the tent with that, to control mud or dust, depending on the weather. It gave the place a pleasant smell and felt good underfoot.

I set about preparing a lunch of fried potatoes and bacon while the men moved the gear inside, and I was overtaken with a sudden hollow feeling.

This was the end of the line for me. I had shepherded my boy to the beginning of the next stage of his life, and from here on I was supernumerary, just a consumer of the goods they would be needing later on.

After lunch, Doc and Chuck went off to find a mule. Daniel and I washed the dishes in uncomfortable silence. He felt it, too.

I skipped all of the things I wanted to say. "Would you come down to the dock with me? I have to book passage." He came along with a silence that a passerby might have mistaken for sullenness. Neither of us really knew what to say. I know that he was glad I was leaving, and felt uncomfortable about that.

It was not a place where you wanted to abandon your only child. The filth and smell bothered me less than the ubiquitous opportunities for sin and excess. I knew him too well to give voice to my concern, but he knew me well enough to read my thoughts.

"Mom," he said as we mounted the steps up to the dock area, "I want you to try not to worry too much about the . . ." His gesture included, as any gesture there would, a number of prostitutes and drunks. "I think I can resist all that."

"I'm more worried about bears and desperados," I said, which at that moment was a lie. "Be careful and watch your temper."

He nodded and smiled. "No more Pinkerton men. Oh . . ." He reached into his deep coat pocket and pulled out the revolver. "We said you would keep this."

I hesitated, but took it. Spinning the universe off in a new direction.

None of the next day's southbound boats was going straight to Sitka, but they all put in at Juneau. I booked on the latest morning one, leaving at ten.

We strolled along the boardwalk for a while, talking about inconsequential things. After a while I told him I could make my own way back to the camp, and had some shopping to do. I gave him a half dollar and bid him pick up a few bottles of beer—not whiskey!

When he was gone, I doubled back to a pawnshop we'd passed. The window was full of trinkets and guns, but there was one thing that had caught my attention as an early Christmas present, a fine hunting knife. From my Philadelphia kitchen I recognized the expensive Toledo steel, the shimmering rainbow of its damascene surface. The handle and hilt were smooth horn and brass. A hefty man's knife, more than a foot from pommel to point.

I bargained the shopkeeper down from fifteen dollars to twelve, which would actually have been a good price back in the States. I also picked up a folding knife for Chuck and a fine tobacco pouch for Doc, soft leather lined with gutta-percha.

Perhaps the knife was a symbolic exchange, weapon for weapon, though I don't think that occurred to me at the time. I just remembered that the steel on his belt knife had been so soft it had bent while he was prising open a crate, and I'd resolved to get him something better.

There was nobody at the tent when I got there, so I put water on to boil and set to scraping the mud off my boots. The straw was luxurious under my bare feet. Nobody could see from the outside, so I left them bare while I padded around preparing dinner. I felt a little exposed and forward when Doc came home, alone, but he glanced at my feet and looked away, and then deliberately removed his own boots and scraped them more or less clean, and set them outside to dry.

He offered to help with dinner, but there was really nothing to do. I was boiling the dried beef into a chewable state. We each got a cup of broth from it, and he told me all about their adventures in mule commerce.

After a few minutes' discourse on mules' teeth and

coats and the mendacity of their owners, a sudden obvious question occurred to me. "Doc—what on earth are you and the boys going to do with a mule? You can't carry it in pieces over the pass."

He blinked a couple of times, sorting that out. "Nobody told you."

"Told me what? About a mule?"

"Rosa . . . things change fast here. We found out this morning that there was a way to bypass the long haul up the mountain."

"On a mule?"

"Not exactly." There was a twinkle in his eye. "An elevator, actually."

I just looked at him. I hadn't seen an elevator since Philadelphia.

"It's in the way of a steam-powered platform, actually, up in Dyea. It'll move half a ton at a time up to the trail on the other side of the pass."

From where we sat, we could see the line of men slowly beetling their way up the stairway cut in the side of Chilkoot Pass. "You mean to tell me all those men haven't heard of it?"

"Likely they can't afford it. Take most of our money."

We both said "But worth it" simultaneously—in my case, a question.

"Without a doubt! We'll be weeks ahead of the others, and fresh—and with a mule and cart to speed us along. Get to the Yukon goldfields before the snow falls. Long before."

My only argument against it was that it sounded too good to be true. "Will you need more money, then?"

"No, Rosa. We have it all calculated."

I plucked at a tent rope. It sang like a bass viol string. "So the tent comes right back down?"

"Not for twelve days. We had to reserve two weeks ahead on the lift." He reached toward me, toward my knee, but stayed his hand halfway. "Stay with us till then?"

So many forces tempted me. But I had already taken my leave emotionally. I didn't want to stitch up the fabric only to tear it apart again.

"I wish . . . no, I have a ticket for Juneau in the morning. And then on to Sitka. I'd better confirm my position at the school there before someone better qualified shows up."

He stared up the road and twice started to speak before words came out. "Before the lads get back, Rosa." He locked his hands between his knees and didn't look at me. "My . . . my regard for you is great, is un-undiminished since . . ."

"Since we talked," I provided. "I feel the same, too, Doc. I'll be waiting for you."

He cleared his throat, got up, and went to the vegetable bag. He took out four large fresh potatoes and a bunch of carrots.

"I was just going to use the dried potatoes."

"Well, it seems to be an occasion." He took the back page of the newspaper and set it on the straw, and laid out the vegetables in a row. He squatted down next to them easily, Indian style, drew out his knife, and tested its edge with his thumb.

"And what will you do if someone else has gotten the job?"

I was sure enough that I hadn't thought too much about it. "If there's nothing in Sitka, I'll probably go back to Juneau, if I can stand the noise."

"Not here, though." He was concentrating on making a long continuous spiral of the potato peel. "Not that I blame you."

"The men on the street are not polite," I said. "They make assumptions."

"I don't think they mean harm."

"Possibly not. But they do harm. I could never feel easy here, the way I did in Sitka."

He nodded. "Not much call for schoolmarms, either, I guess."

"Probably not." I'd seen a handbill, actually, advertising for a grade school teacher. *Who would bring young children to this place?* was my first thought, but then I realized they wouldn't be stampeders' children. There might be a thousand people living here permanently.

But the salary was laughable, given the expense of living at this far end of civilization, and I had little experience with children so young. Only Sunday school, where even the most mischievous could endure being good for an hour because Jesus is watching and cookies are waiting at the end of it.

"Glad you're not going back to Seattle anymore."

"It's not close enough." though it was my safety net, if nothing in Alaska worked.

"You'll write once you have an address?"

"Of course. You'll probably still be waiting here. At least I hope it won't be two weeks before I'm settled in."

He looked up at a noise I hadn't heard. "The lads coming." Down at the far end of the road, I could see them leading a mule with a cart.

"How long are you going to give it?" I asked. "If you don't pan out."

"Quit after the first million, that's my only plan. No call to be greedy."

"Suppose the raven was right?"

"The raven?"

"The one on the boat, who said 'no gold.'"

"He was just croakin'."

"It sounded clear to me."

He laughed nervously. "Rosa, I'd never take you to be superstitious. Birds don't talk."

Our eyes met. "This one did, Doc. You heard it as clearly as I did." I almost told him about the other two times, but the boys were approaching.

They introduced us to the mule, which they had named Dr. Jekyll, reserving Mr. Hyde for when he misbehaved. While they were freeing him of his traces I fed him a double handful of oats, enjoying the feel of his soft whiskery mouth and smooth hard teeth.

He did host an entourage of flies and lesser creatures, but he didn't smell bad for a mule, and he had large sad eyes. They tied him up to a tent post, and then thought better of it—he might decide to take the tent for a walk—and just looped the rope twice around a large rock.

In the cart they had twenty-two bottles of beer, having consumed two on the way; a roll of mosquito netting, and a small wooden cask of sherry from Spain. Doc was exasperated at the expense—and the fact that they had spent the money without consulting him or me—but we all mellowed with a cup of the stuff, a sweet powerful dark syrup. It was called "oloroso," a sad-sounding name for a merry libation.

I spiced up the beef stew with some of the sherry and sharp Colman's mustard, and we enjoyed it over thick slabs of sourdough bread. We had some of the beer with it, too, and the talk was lively. I wondered aloud about how amazed I would have been twenty years ago, a proper Wellesley girl, to see a vision of myself in the future, covered with grime and swatting mosquitoes, drinking beer with a trio of disreputable prospectors in a mudhole at the end of the world. A master of celestial mechanics stranded at a place where the night was so short you hardly saw the stars.

Chuck allowed that he couldn't do anything about the stars, but he had seen a place that advertised hot baths for two bits, open all day and night, a barber shop on Third Street.

That wasn't so far away. I produced a silver dollar and said I would treat us all to at least one evening of cleanliness.

They insisted on bringing Dr. Jekyll and his cart along, so I wouldn't have to walk through the mud on the way back. I protested on the poor beast's behalf, but common sense could not penetrate their chivalry.

The town was lively, a honky-tonk piano banging away in the place that used to be Soapy Smith's saloon, competing with a couple of banjo players on the boardwalk, rolling their eyes in blackface while a Negro child danced loudly on a piece of tin, holding out a hat as we passed by. Farther down the street, a supposedly dancing bear sat and glared at the human who held his leash and poked him with a cane. Dr. Jekyll froze at the sight or smell of him, which gave Doc an opportunity to demonstrate his way with animals: he stood between the mule and the bear and stroked his ears and talked quietly to him, and got him to turn around and seek a less direct route to Third Street.

Charlie's Barber Shop advertised three metal tubs in back. We tied up the mule and followed the red arrows to a door that had a picture of a man in a tub scrubbing himself with a brush and whistling. Inside, two woodstoves glowed dull red with the effort of keeping large pails of water hot. It was a pleasant smell, resin from the fuel sticks of pine scrap mixed with the steam and hot metal and soap perfume.

Two Chinese children were in charge of the enterprise. The girl took me by the hand and, carrying a candle, led me to a curtain, which she parted to reveal a sit-down bath of galvanized metal. She lit four candles around the tub and showed me the dressing corner—clothes hanger on a rod, a chair, and a mat for dirty boots. The wooden floor was otherwise clean. She poured two buckets of water in the tub and said, "I get hot, you undress."

I'd had a bath less than a week before, in the Sitka rooming house, but was due for another. I took off my clothes and didn't need a mirror to see that I was a comical sight, hopelessly begrimed everywhere I'd been exposed to Skagway; white as milk otherwise.

The girl brought in the steaming water and giggled at me, whether out of embarrassment or at my ridiculous aspect I didn't know. She poured the water in the tub and told me to get in; she'd bring another in five minutes.

It was tepid but wonderful. The soap was a sharp-edged homemade block that smelled of both bacon fat and lavender, so I guess I did, too.

She brought the second bucket and rinsed my soapy hair with it, and then I lay back and luxuriated in the lightness and warmth of it.

We take bathing for granted nowadays, and no doubt society is healthier as well as prettier for the casual frequency of it. But with every gain there's a loss, in this case the special time-out-of-time transportation, warm water in the flickering darkness.

When the water cooled to around body temperature I got out and dried off with a rough towel, and for the first time had the sensation that I was being watched. It would not have been hard to put a peephole in the curtain, or more than one, invisible in the darkness. Were lonely prospectors staring at my unremarkable body? I had an odd feeling about that, a thimbleful of outrage mixed with a cup of amusement. Dressing, I put on a little show for my invisible and probably nonexistent audience, which caused me to glow with embarrassment. I was still glowing when I emerged—Doc, who had just come from his own bath, commented on my healthy color.

He and I sat on a bench outside while the boys bathed. The smoke from his pipe seemed to keep the mosquitoes away.

Out of nowhere—out of "left field," as they say now—he asked me about God. I said something conventional about God helping me through my sadness, which was true.

"You say sadness, but never 'grief,'" he said. "And you never speak about your late husband."

I was almost cornered into telling the truth. Since Doc did speak often, and lovingly, about his lost Lilian, my reticence about Edward must have seemed strange.

"It was not a happy union," I said. "In fact, it was as much a deliverance as a loss. As if God had given us freedom."

"He was bad to Daniel, too?" he asked.

"Very bad." I couldn't elaborate, of course.

"Daniel never speaks of him, either." He paused to fiddle with his pipe, waiting for me to say something more. I had a sudden insight that almost made me laugh out loud: Doc suspected that there had never *been* an Edward; that Daniel was a love child, conceived in sin. "He only talks about his early childhood."

"His father was very sick for a long time before he died," I said. "Perhaps he doesn't want to talk about it. I know I don't."

"Forgive me. I'm being nosy."

"You have the right," I said. "Why did you ask about God?"

He scraped a match alight along the bench—were they still called "lucifers" then?—and twirled it to burn off the sulfur before he puffed his pipe alight.

"Maybe for reassurance. He seems distant." He turned to spit politely. "It wasn't this way on the farm. Maybe we shouldn't of left."

"How do you mean?"

He was quiet for a long spell. I remember the tinkling piano and distant drunken laughter.

"God was always there on the farm. Is that simpleminded? In the season's changing, the lambs and calves. Even the bad times. The drought, the locust summer—that was like the Bible; we were being tested. Sooner or later the rain came back, the insects died.

"But lately I doubt. I lie awake in the middle of the night and doubt that He's there, and ask for a sign. Nothing comes."

"God doesn't work that way."

"So they say. So they say. But you follow that around; how does anybody know how God works? He could send a sign by lifting His little finger. And maybe save my soul. Is it worth that little?"

"Maybe the raven was a sign."

He laughed. "A real sign. Something clear."

"I can give you the Sunday school answer. God gave us the capacity to doubt as the ultimate test of our faith. If God sent you a sign, then believing would be easy. It's not supposed to be easy."

"I know the Sunday school answer. What's Rosa's answer?"

I should not have calculated my response. I should

have told him about my own sleepless nights, full of nothingness. Instead, I asked him whether he had heard of Pascal's Wager. He hadn't.

"Pascal asks you to imagine two worlds: one where God exists, and one where He doesn't.

"Suppose you live out your life according to God's precepts, and when you die, it turns out there is nothing afterwards; you just cease to exist."

"You'll have wasted a lot of time in church."

"Yes, but only that. And if there *is* a God, you will have gained an eternity of bliss.

"But suppose the opposite—suppose you assume there is no God, and act only according to whim and appetite. When you die, if you're right, nothing will happen. If you're wrong, though, you will have bartered a few years of pleasure for an eternity of damnation."

He nodded into the darkness. "Forever is a long time, compared to the rest of your life. That's what his argument boils down to."

"And it's not as if faith could not be a source of pleasure, either," I began.

"But wait," he said. "I'm a plain and practical man. I don't like loose ends, but that's all your Mr. Pascal offers. You have to *die* to collect on his bet."

"But living a life of faith is an end in itself."

He wagged his head and smiled. "So is a life of dissipation, is it not? Little as you and I know about it."

I laughed with him. "You wicked, wicked man!" The boys came out of their baths then, ending that line of conversation before it could become dangerous. But a seed had been sown.

They set me on Dr. Jekyll's cart, and I rolled through the streets of Skagway like royalty, or an invalid. The boys were redolent of whiskey as well as soap, and treated us to their versions of "Clementine" and "Sweet Betsy from Pike."

I resolved to give Daniel a good talking-to the next morning, but by morning I had no pinnacle to climb. While the boys snored sonorously, Doc and I shared intercourse, twice. It was a desperate, wonderful thing. If God and Pascal were looking down on the two of us, wrapped in mildewed blankets, caught in the cage of each other's limbs, they must have understood, if not forgiven.

After nine decades of thought and prayer, I am all but certain that God forgives transgressions of that nature. I even dare to think that sometimes He precipitates them, for His mysterious reasons.

The parting.

The morning was difficult. Maybe it was guilt on my part, but I was certain that Daniel and Chuck knew exactly what their parents had been up to during the night—and morning. I could certainly see the difference in Doc, and didn't dare look in a mirror myself.

The marriage obligation had never been pleasurable with Edward, and of course it wasn't unusual for a woman of my time to believe that that was normal. But my less complete surrender to Doc on the boat, before Sitka, had been almost frightening in its intense pleasure, and this was even greater, amplified by the desperation of parting. (A practical side of me must acknowledge that he knew more about a woman's anatomy and nervous system than I did, despite all my formal education. Three cheers for veterinary science and none for Wellesley.)

While breakfast was cooking, I passed around the early Christmas presents. Daniel and Chuck were thrilled with their knives, and Doc impressed with the gutta-percha tobacco pouch, the like of which he'd never seen.

I said good-bye to Doc and Chuck at the tent, giving Doc a chaste kiss and a whispered promise, and walked to the boat with Daniel. I tried not to say anything too mother-hennish, and neither of us cried until the whistle blew and the boat drifted away from the dock.

He waved until the boat turned into the channel. I climbed up a deck and could see him again, but he was walking down the street by then, head down and hands in pockets.

I couldn't ignore the possibility that this was the last time I would see my son, but that seemed remote. He was in good hands.

There was no place to sit on the small boat's bow, but I passed a lot of time there anyhow, standing with my weight against the worn mahogany rail. The wind of our passage was bracing—salt and pine, fish and kelp—and I floated in my freedom, a feeling that was both pleasant and disturbing: for the first time in my adult life, I was truly alone. Parents gone, husband a bad memory, son on his own path. In a way, I was a new person, reborn.

• • •

My layover in noisy Juneau was a mercifully short four hours. I could have gone aboard the steamboat to wait, but instead bought my ticket and checked my trunk, and then worked my way up the muddy boardwalk toward the tea shop that had Edison and Scott Joplin. On the way, I stopped in a newsstand-bookshop and bought a volume called *Northwest Indian Ways*, about the Tlingit and Haida races.

The men who had seemed so rough and frightening a few days before had suddenly become well-dressed gentlemen, after Skagway. They wore or carried guns but also tipped their hats to me.

The toothless proprietor greeted me warmly and asked after "my husband," and I said he was my fiancé, off to find his fortune in the goldfields. His face grew grave at that, and he wished us both luck.

I read for a couple of hours, fascinated especially by the tales that form the basis of the Tlingit religion, which read like Aesop's fables, except that the morals at the end are often alien; sometimes brutal.

Half of them have the Raven as a character, a kind of trickster like Loki, and the only creature who can talk to both humans and animals. That gave me a chill to read.

He figured in a myth reminiscent of both the Tower of Babel and the biblical flood: long ago all the animals and people could talk together, but then the world was flooded in a great rain, and each kind of human and animal wound up on its own island. With the passage of time, each one developed its own language, which none of the others could understand except for the Raven, who flew from island to island, and could take the shape of any creature. So ravens have those talents to this day, shape-changing and speech.

Then, out of the corner of my eye, I saw a sudden motion. On the other side of the window, a raven had landed on the boardwalk. That gave me a terrible start. But of course they were not uncommon in Juneau.

He did look at me, though, or so it seemed. Then he hobbled down the boardwalk a couple of yards and took off when a cowboy-looking fellow aimed a boot at him.

Oddly enough, the bird circled around and landed back outside the window again. I set the book aside and did a quick drawing of him in my diary.

Then I realized I'd better be getting down to the boat if I wanted to secure an outside seat; I'd want to sleep during the trip, and that wouldn't be comfortable, sandwiched between two strangers. So I paid my bill and plugged up my ears and stepped outside.

A raven was waiting for me. The same one? It hopped out of my way, into the mud, but didn't fly away. At least it didn't say anything. Absurdly, I could feel its eyes on my back as I made my way down the steep hill.

The beginning of the end.

I did secure an end seat, but slept little, even though I made bold to buy a whiskey with hot water at the lunch counter. So much was going through my mind, about both Sitka and Skagway, future and past. Reading would not quiet my hopes and worries, nor would the dramatic scenery distract me. When darkness crept upon us, I listened to my fellow travelers' snores and crepitations for two or three hours.

It seemed as if the ice was somewhat thicker now at the Icy Strait, looking curiously warm in the rising sun's crimson light. Twice we thumped against small ice floes.

Rain began soon after that, and it poured all the way to Sitka. I was glad not to be shivering on deck, but had improvidentially left my umbrella in the trunk, to which I was not allowed access en route.

So I was thoroughly drenched by the time I arrived at the Baranoff Hotel. The sour old lady softened enough to seat me in a wicker rocking chair by the fire, and bring me a pot of tea. The tea and pine smoke restored my spirit. I arranged for laundry so I would be presentable for Reverend Bower the next day.

It was a four-hour cleaning service, so I went to my room and read and napped, sleeping deeply for the first time since Juneau's din had been replaced by the steamer's chuffing and churning.

The book gave me strange dreams about gageets, the supernatural creatures who were half human, half sea otter—tall and skinny, covered with fur, arms growing out of their chests. They are soul-stealers, kidnapping the spirits of incautious people on or near the water. I dreamed the boat from Juneau was full of them, and the pilot was a raven with long legs and a captain's hat. At the Icy Strait we turned seaward, toward the glittering glaciers, and when I tried to protest, two of the gageets held me fast. In my diary I wrote that one had the face of Edward and the other was the toothless tea shop man.

I turned to the Bible that night, reading stories about sons. Joseph and his coat of many colors, the prodigal son, Abraham and Isaac. Nothing about a woman who abandoned her son, leaving him to wander in the wilderness.

Or did Mary do that? Allowing her Son the freedom to go and seek His death.

The next day, Thursday, I presented myself to Reverend Bower precisely at nine. He was glad to see me.

"I sent a letter to Skagway," he said, enclosing my hand between his fat warm palms, "but of course you wouldn't have gotten it yet."

I nodded. "The line at the post office was so long and unruly, I left it alone. I thought if I didn't have a job here, I could keep looking."

"Look no further. The board was glad to accept you. Here." He shuffled over to a closet and brought out a potato sack full of books and papers. "I took the liberty of assembling this, against the possibility of your return. It's copies of the students' texts, and some material about Alaskan history." He hoisted the bag up onto his desk, and stacked up the books.

None of them presented much of a challenge except for Latin. In Kansas there'd been a separate instructor for that. I picked the book up and opened it here and there, feeling vague echoes of panic and shame from high school and college. "Not my best subject," I said ruefully. It hadn't been on the test.

He took it from my hand and riffled through the beginning. "Don't worry about it. Only three boys are taking it, and I've been guiding them through. You'd be better off studying Tlingit."

"Can white people actually speak it?" The glossary in the back of my book was full of unpronounceable words.

"It does take practice, and I suppose they laugh at our accents. You'll have some help from one of their elders, a shaman we call Gordon. Less help from the Russian Orthodox priest. He speaks it pretty well, but wants their children to learn Russian."

"That's the young man who conducted the funeral?" He nodded. "But he didn't seem to speak much Russian himself, except for liturgy."

He spread his hands. "What can you say? He came from San Francisco, born there, but his parents are Russian and he felt a vocation. Perhaps mixed with a little guilt."

"So I'll be in competition with him?"

"No, he's just a gadfly, an anachronism. Only old folks speak Russian anymore. Ah, Gordon."

I hadn't heard him enter the room. But I smelled him, wood smoke and must. He was wearing jeans and a flannel shirt, but also had a kind of bib of bones and shells and feathers woven together.

His face was burnt-bronze and heavily creased; he could have been forty or seventy. There was a little gray in the hair plaited into a large topknot. He regarded me with cool intelligence.

"This is Mrs. Flammarion, our new teacher for the older students."

He touched my hand with his calloused one. "You will also be at the mission," he said with very little accent.

"That's right." His face was gentle but his eyes bored into me.

"I'll see you there, then."

"Gordon's a shaman, trying to understand our strange ways."

"Very strange," he said, smiling, still looking at me. Then he turned to Reverend Bower. "Those poppies along the north wall are not going to thrive. They were planted too late, and don't get enough sun anyhow."

"Can you transplant them?"

"Around to the front, some of them. Replace them with some things from the forest."

"Fine. Thank you." Gordon turned and walked away.

"Your gardener's a shaman?" I asked.

"The other way around, I suppose. He's a shaman who took an interest in our garden. Walked in one day about a year ago and told me what needed to be done. Works a couple of days a week, fifty cents a day, and he's magical with plants."

"And he comes to the mission school?"

He nodded. "Sunday school. Sits in the back and listens; never says anything. There for English, rather than religion, I think. He's a strange bird, but pleasant enough."

Mr. Bower left me in the office for awhile to read the two contracts, church and state, binding me to Sitka for two years. If the boys came back with pockets bulging, I supposed I could leave behind the $180 a month.

School didn't start until September here, so I had more than a month to study Alaskan history and make up my lesson plans. For the other subjects, I could adapt my Kansan lessons, which I could teach nearly by heart. It was the same four grades, with fewer students.

I looked up at a light tapping on the doorjamb and was surprised to see Gordon rather than Reverend Bower.

"May I help you?"

"Perhaps we can help each other, Mrs. Flammarion. As we're both instructing the young." He went on to explain that on Sunday evenings most of the Tlingit children came to his place for instruction in their own ways.

It was partly language instruction. Even the ones who spoke Tlingit at home tended to speak English among themselves—some a mixture of Russian and English, which was not music to his ears. His parents' generation had fought the Russians, and the invaders had killed many of his "uncles." (I think in Tlingit the word included a larger group of men than his parents' siblings.)

He offered the children instruction in the old tales and ways, saying everything twice, first in Tlingit and then in English. Would I be willing to come and help him with the translation? The Sunday school teacher who had left hadn't wanted to do it, and Gordon was afraid he was teaching them bad English.

His English was really rather good, considering, but it sounded like a wonderful opportunity for me, so I agreed immediately. He took a stub of pencil and drew a map, and told me to come at around sundown Sunday; remember to bring a lamp.

It was only after he'd left that I wondered quite what I was getting into. Did he really need a translator, or was I being used for some less obvious purpose?

When Reverend Bower came back in, he clarified the situation a little. The previous Sunday school teacher *had* given it a try, but he hadn't lasted an hour: the hut where Gordon instructed the young smelled so bad he couldn't breathe, and left in fear of becoming physically ill in front of them.

"Perhaps women are stronger in that regard than men," I said. "Babies aren't bouquets of posies."

He was amused at that. "We shall see, we shall see. I'm sure you'll find it interesting, though in a way it's counter to our basic charge here."

"Because we're supposed to convert them, and not the other way around?"

"Oh, I'm not afraid that Gordon's going to convert you to paganism. But you're right; our job is to Christianize and civilize the youngsters. Gordon's no ally there."

"So I'll be a spy in the enemy's lair. I like that image."

"Indeed. Maybe you can learn their tales well enough to portray them in a Christian light and use them in Sunday school."

"Maybe." The ones I'd read didn't have much potential.

We finished the paperwork and Reverend Bower gave me a twenty-dollar advance, which I didn't need but didn't refuse. I took his advice and went down to the newspaper office, where there was a bulletin board with notices of rooms and homes to rent and buy.

There was a room only a block from school, which would be handy in rain and snow. But I was intrigued by a one-room cottage being built on the edge of town, a small log cabin. A hundred-dollar deposit would secure it for me.

The rain had stopped, so I followed directions out to the lot and found them working there, a white man and a Negro assisted by two Tlingit boys.

The short muscular Negro, Saul Johnson, owned the lot. So far the cottage was nothing but a cleared area with three courses of logs laid around a simple stone fireplace and a doorway, but he showed me the plans and said I would be able to move in in three or four weeks.

I wasn't sure they could do that, but the place was hard to resist, surrounded on three sides by forest, the front porch looking out over the bay and mountains. You could smell salt on the breeze.

I gave him half the hundred-dollar down payment, the other half due when I moved in. Walking back down the hill, I wondered whether I had been too impulsive, and decided not. Besides the reasonable price, the quiet setting, and the lovely view, I was excited at the prospect of moving into a place that was all my own, with no previous inhabitants. It was a first for me, and at forty years of age, about time.

(The next day Mr. Bower expressed surprise that a Southern lady would enter into a contract with a Negro man. I asked him whether *he* would and he said yes, probably; Mr. Johnson was new in town but had a good reputation as a worker. I didn't pursue it beyond that, I hope leaving him slightly embarrassed. In fact, the only two people I missed from our life in Philadelphia were Negroes, Sue Anne and Jimmy.)

My rented room was small and close, so I spent most of my days in the school library, working on my lesson plans but also idly reading. When the weather was fine—not often!—I would go outside to draw and paint, knowing there would be little time for that after school started.

Letters, leavings.

It was almost three weeks before I got a letter from Daniel. It had been twelve days in transit, which I would come to regard as swift, and was crumpled and mud-stained but legible.

They had made good time after the "elevator" had lifted them and the mule up to the top of the pass, and at his writing had just arrived at the Yukon River. There were boats and rafts for sale, but at ridiculous prices, so they'd begun collecting materials for a steerable raft.

He didn't say whether they planned to negotiate

the river with a mule on board. I wouldn't want to be the mule—or the people!

They were all in good health and had had no trouble with the other adventurers; in fact, there was a friendly spirit of cooperation amongst most of them. Everybody in it together and plenty of gold to go around. I suspected it would be more competitive when they actually arrived in the Yukon goldfields.

The Sunday school was an odd challenge. I had both whites and Tlingits, from age five or six on up. Most were under fifteen, but there were several adults of both races the first couple of weeks, obviously making sure I was worthy of their children.

And Gordon, always coming in a little late, standing silently in the rear.

No one paid closer attention than he. He never spoke, but it was not—as some of the adults must have thought—either deference or contempt. He was there to observe, and he missed nothing.

The evening sessions led by Gordon were fascinating. He rarely went longer than an hour, often stopping in midstory, leaving us hanging till next week. The parables were amusing, sometimes fantastic, sometimes more or less down to earth, about what happens if you don't follow tribal rules—"sin and suffer," as we say.

After a month or so, though, I realized there was a big difference between his stories and the ones I told in Sunday school: his weren't "sin and suffer; then see the error of your ways and become a better person." His were "do the wrong thing and pay for it," period, as often as not with death. They reminded me strongly of Edgar Allan Poe's macabre tales.

I could sympathize with the fellow who took a whiff of the inside of the hut and fled back to civilization. It was pretty abominable, but I'd been living in close quarters with a bunch of prospectors, who aren't exactly dainty. The human smell didn't bother me so much as the rancid seal oil they used for lighting—and when the weather got cold that would be doubled and redoubled by the smell of their parkas, sealskins poorly cured and worn inside out.

You really can get used to almost anything, though, and the discomfort I endured was more than paid back by the respect I got from the children. While it lasted.

Many of Gordon's stories were about the Raven, who was a trickster, but also a sort of Prometheus figure—he tricked the various gods and titans into giving up the sun, fire, and, most of all, the tides, so the sea would yield its bounty. These stories didn't have people in them, except as godlike personifications.

One story that still haunts me, though, had only people, and a mysterious machine.

Two women went up into the mountains to gather berries, leaving the rest of the tribe on shore. They were repairing boats and nets, drying fish, and so forth. It was a lovely clear day, and the children were playing on the beach.

Coming from far away, a large kite drifted toward the shore, trailing a long tail that almost reached the ground. One of the children chased after it, but once he took hold, it lifted him off the ground. His playmates tried to drag him back to earth, at first playfully, and then in earnest. It lifted them off the ground, too.

The men looked up from their boats and nets, hearing the children's fearful cries, and ran to rescue them. One by one, they also were lifted from the shore. The women saw what was happening, and abandoned their food preparation to try to drag the men and children back down. All of them were pulled up into the sky as well, and rose toward the sun and out of sight.

The two women who had been gathering berries in the mountains came back down to this mysterious sight: the camp was completely deserted, but there was no sign of violence. Evening fell and then the morning came, and they were still alone. They assumed that some supernatural force had taken the tribe away, and they would just have to wait until it, or some other force, brought them back.

They continued the routine business of staying alive, gathering shellfish and roots and berries. It soon became obvious that one was pregnant, which was a mystery, since she had not been with a man. It turned out that she had been impregnated by a magical seed she had eaten in the forest.

She gave birth to a boy, and the women were determined to raise him the right way to become a powerful shaman, which was arduous. Every morning he bathed in icy water. He scourged himself with branches and purged his body with strong herbs.

At a young age he began lifting rocks on the beach, larger and larger ones. Finally he was even able to tip the largest boulder, just by planting his feet and giving it all the strength he could muster.

When he was barely the age of a man, one of the women, now old, saw a sight she couldn't believe: From far out to sea, a kite drifted toward shore, carrying on its long tail all the missing tribe. She called to the boy, and he ran down to the shore to meet it.

When it was directly over him, he grabbed the feet of the lowest woman. The kite tried to lift him off the ground, but he fought back with all his might.

Just when it seemed he was about to be defeated, his feet began to grow roots—his father had been a tree, after all—and they went deeper and deeper, holding the kite fast while the women, and then the men, and then the children, climbed down to safety. The boy released the kite, and it drifted off into the sky.

End of story. I asked Gordon whether the members of the tribe had aged while they were in the air, and he said no; the children were still children. Where did he think they had gone? He laughed and said, "Someplace that was not here."

Of course, at the simplest level, the story is just a Tlingit version of "say your prayers, obey your elders, eat your vegetables; grow up strong and good." But that's not really what it's about. It's a mystery tale, about life and loss. And, I've come to believe, it's about not needing to understand.

When Gordon recited the story, surrounded by rapt children in that dim fetid hut, I had the feeling he was telling it to me; for me. A few months later, I would know that that was true.

School started in September, and I was soon immersed in a hectic but satisfying routine. The white boys and girls at Sheldon Jackson came to learn trades as well as the conventional three Rs; the Tlingit school, which grew out of the Presbyterian mission, was primarily a trade school, with a little book-learning thrown in.

I divided my labors between the two. For four days of the week, I taught high school courses in the concrete octagon of Sheldon Jackson. Fridays, I went to the Sitka Industrial Training School, where the boys studied carpentry, machine work, and carving; the girls learned to sew and cook and clean. For a short while, they could put down their tools and pick up books, a change of pace that was appreciated and resented by about equal numbers.

At Industrial, a lot of my work was elementary, making up for what the Tlingit children had not learned. I made sure they could parse sentences and do outlines, both of which seemed foreign to their nature, and had them write book reports that they would have to read in front of the classroom. Just like their white counterparts, some hated it and some were natural hams. It was funny to see the influence of Gordon on some of them, speaking in a low, serious voice; punctuating their talk with sweeping gestures.

Every week or two I got letters from Daniel or Doc. It was obviously real labor for Doc, a neat printed text deeply grooved by his pressure on the pencil. Daniel's letters started out chatty and long, describing life in the camp and Dawson City. As winter fell, his notes grew short and almost terse.

Their claim was about fifteen miles out of town, on Gold Run Creek. With all three of them working, they were just staying ahead of their expenses, but a lot of their time in September and October had gone toward building a makeshift cabin sturdy enough to get them through the arctic cold. Their first snowfall was in September, and though they preferred it to the rain, they knew what was coming. The ground would be frozen rock-hard, and to run it through the sluice they'd have to pour buckets of boiling water on it.

Still, Doc especially was cautiously optimistic. Several people had made rich strikes on the creek, within a mile or so of their claim. Patience and hard work would do it.

I wished that Daniel would echo the sentiment.

My own cabin was finished on time, and it was a pleasant refuge from Sitka's gray cold and nearly constant rain. I had minimal furnishings—table, chair, bed, wardrobe, and bookshelf—but they were adequate. If I'd had guests, they would have to sit on food crates or the footlocker I'd carried all the way from Philadelphia.

That was one thing that sustained me. As simple and crude as my surroundings were, they were heaven compared to the cold and perverse servitude I'd endured in that huge mansion. At another level, not as silly as it may sound, anyone who's gone through the protracted anxiety of preparing and hosting a formal dinner for twenty can take real pleasure in dumping a can of beans into a tin pan and warming it in the fireplace.

By November, I was in a state that might be called extreme happiness punctuated by occasional despair. (The doctor I would have twenty years later would nod wisely and say "manic-depressive.") The school and missionary work were both going well. I had a basic vocabulary of Tlingit—far more than most whites managed, or bothered, to do. The children responded in a spirit of fun, acting as affectionate tutors.

But I was worried about my boys, worried sick, as winter closed in. Daniel no longer told me how many ounces per week they were extracting, which I assumed meant there were none. They spent a lot of time scavenging for wood to burn, and were eating nothing that they hadn't carried up. Doc said they might sell the mule, because there was no forage for it and feed was dear. That would seriously isolate them; fifteen miles through snow was a long haul.

As winter deepened my mood darkened. The days were short and cold; I would leave for school in the dark and return to the cabin in the dark. I was facing my first Christmas without family. Reverend Bower sympathized; he said his own first Alaska winter had been terrible. But you grew to like them. If you survived the first one, I thought.

My world fell apart first by degrees, and then by sudden shock.

The Tlingit children stopped coming to Sunday school. When I went to Gordon's Sunday sessions, they would avoid me.

They even stopped coming to the Tlingit school on Fridays, the day I taught there. Mr. Bower and the sheriff went through the village door to door and told everyone that the parents could be fined if the children didn't attend.

I asked Gordon to find out what was going on, and he traced it to an unexpected source: Dmitri Popovitch, the Russian priest. Evidently jealous of my success, he had intimated to his old-lady congregation that the source of my power was unnatural. I was a witch.

In a Tlingit family, when a grandmother lays down the law, you obey her. Gordon said he would try to talk some sense into the women. A shaman's word should mean more to them than a priest's.

While this was going on, the worst storm of the

year piled snow on ice while I taught the last day of class before Christmas. On the way home I fell several times, and arrived at the cabin sore and soaked and freezing.

I bolted the door behind me and crossed the room slowly, groping, to the table where I felt candle and matches. With one match I lit the candle and a couple of peg lamps, and then the main kerosene lamp, for its smoky warmth. When I went back to snuff the peg lamps, I saw that I'd trod upon a letter that had been slid under the door.

It was from the Yukon Territory, the address barely legible, a pencil scrawl unlike Daniel's schoolboy hand or Doc's careful printing.

With curiosity rather than premonition, I took a paring knife and slit open the worn foolscap and carried its scrawled message back to the lamp. It was from Chuck. The letter is long since gone, but I think I have the wording set in my memory:

Mrs. Flammarion, both my Pa and your son are murdered. A drunkard fell upon Pa on the street in Dawson City, thinking him someone else, and when Dan went to his aid the drunk shot them both with a pistol. When he seen what he had done he shot his own self, but not to much effect, and he will be hung this week. But my Pa and Dan died right there, shot in the heart and the head, while I was out at the claim, and by the time someone got me the terrible news and I got me into the town, they was both froze solid in back of the doctor's office. I don't know no way to tell this to make it gentle. It's the worst thing that ever happened.

I didn't burst into tears or scream or rend my garments. I sat there in the sputtering light and read the note again, sure that it must be some cruel trick or stupid joke. I had sure knowledge that Chuck could not write much beyond signing his name. But then I turned over the paper and found a note in the same hand:

"*Writ this 14th day of December year of our Lord 1898 by Morris Chambers, for the hand of Chuck Coleman, his mark here.* And there was Chuck's scrawl with this note appended beneath: *I was not there at the time but hear tell that your son was very brave. My gravest condolences in your loss. M.C.*

Then I was blinded by tears and collapsed, striking my head on the pine floor, and then striking it again and again, hard bright sparks in my eyes. I rolled on the floor weeping, and lost my water, beyond care.

I remembered the moment in Skagway when he handed me the Pinkerton man's revolver, agreeing with some reluctance that he should never need it.

I needed it now.

I staggered to the dresser by the bed and jerked open the top drawer. There it was in a corner, wrapped in blue muslin. I unwrapped it, sudden oil smell, and verified that it was loaded, and raised it to my temple. Then I thought about the horrible sight that would leave, and lowered the muzzle to where I thought my heart was, beneath my left breast, and a large raven came through the door.

The door didn't open. He walked through it as if it were made of air. "Rosa," he said in a clear voice, "you can't do that. Your God would not approve."

He stalked across the floor in that determined way that ravens have. "One Corinthians, chapter six: 'know thee not that your body is the temple of the Holy Ghost, which is in you . . . and ye are not your own?'"

With a clatter of feathers, he hopped up onto the dresser. "Chapter twenty of Exodus. Verse thirteen. You must know that one."

"What are you?"

"A raven, dummy. Exodus 20:13. Give it to me."

"You're the one who kept telling me 'no gold'?"

"Yes. Exodus 20:13?"

"'Thou shalt not kill.'"

"Let's get that straight. It doesn't say, 'Thou shalt not kill anybody but yourself.'"

I turned the gun on it. "It does tell us that the Devil quotes scripture."

"Luke. And you're gonna kill the Devil with an eggbeater."

The gun was suddenly light in my hand. I looked down and it was an eggbeater. I dropped it and it hit the floor with a loud thump, and formed back into a revolver.

"Not that I'm actually the Devil. I'm not actually even a raven." It hopped to the floor, impossibly slow, and for an instant turned into old Gordon. He had his huge nest of hair let down, all the way to his knees, and was wearing nothing else. He turned back into the raven.

"You're Gordon?"

"No and yes. You know what the Tlingit raven is."

"A shape-changer. But—"

"And a creature who can talk to all animals, including humans. Leave it at that, for the time being."

I picked up the letter and turned it over, to the terrible message. "You have something to do with this?"

"I didn't cause it. I'm here because of it, of course."

"To save me . . . from myself?"

"I haven't saved you yet."

I groped for the chair behind me, and sat down. I couldn't speak; couldn't even think. "What do you really look like, if you aren't a bird or Gordon?"

It flickered, like a candle flame, but didn't change.

"In a sense, the question is meaningless; I take whatever form is appropriate. I do have a shape for resting, but I think it would disturb you."

"Demonic?"

"No. Forget demons and gods. It's as plain and natural as changing clothes. Stand up."

I did, and suddenly the room around me changed. I could see three walls at once, in sharp detail even though the light was low and flickering. My eyes were only about three feet off the ground. Effortlessly, I turned my head completely around, and saw on the wall behind me the shadow of a large bird.

"What?" I said, and it came out both a word and a squawk.

"You're a bald eagle," it said. "Come over to the mirror."

Walking was strange, bobbing talons scraping

along the wood. In the full-length mirror by the wardrobe, the image of a magnificent eagle, cocking its head when I cocked mine; raising and lowering its feet. I raised my arm and spread my fingers; it raised a wing and the end feathers spread out. My mind and body knew exactly how that would change my course of flight, scooping air to slow and drop.

It was a strange mental state, simple and beautiful. I tried to say something about that, but all that came out was another squawk: "I am!"

"You certainly are." The eagle in the mirror stretched impossibly tall and with a little "pop," turned back into me, nude. I covered myself reflexively, as if a crow or demon would care, and clothes appeared on my flesh.

Nothing like normal clothing, though. I looked at my strange image in the mirror: it looked as if I had been dipped in wax, a garment like a second skin, covering everything but my head, hands, and feet. Slippers appeared on my feet.

"That will keep you warm. Follow me." He walked through the door, again without opening it.

"But . . ." I blew out the lights and pushed open the door. It had stopped snowing, and the raven was standing there in the moonlight.

It was bitter cold, but the suit of clothes warmed up automatically. It also warmed my face and hands somehow. I touched my face and it felt slippery.

"This way." It hopped and fluttered down the path at the rate of a fast walk. We went away from town, up the hill toward Mount Verstovaia.

I followed him without question, numb and confused. We walked down a game trail for a few hundred yards—I was starting to worry about bears—and then picked our way through undergrowth for a few minutes.

The raven said something in a language neither bird nor human, and a door opened in the middle of the air. I stepped sideways and saw that there was nothing behind it. The door was a rectangle of soft golden light that led into a room that was manifestly *not there*. But the raven walked in, and I cautiously followed him.

The floor of the room was soft, the air warm with a trace of something like cinnamon. As if someone had been baking rolls.

The door closed and the raven disappeared. I think I did, too. At least I had no sense of being in any one place—all of the room seemed equally close. Perhaps I became the room, in some sense.

"I want to go a few places," the raven said in my mind, "and show you a few things. You've read *Gulliver's Travels*."

"Yes, I have."

"Wasn't a question. This is not that. But there may be some aspects of if you will find amusing, or educational."

A rush of anxiety finally caught up with me. "I don't want to go anyplace. I want to go home, and sort things out."

"You'll get home. Right now I want to put some distance between you and that revolver."

"That was a rash impulse. I won't do it." As I said that, I wondered whether it was a lie.

"You'll be home in less than no time. Close your eyes until I tell you to open them."

I obeyed for a couple of minutes, though it was extremely uncomfortable—as if I were being rotated slowly about one axis, like a leisurely figure skater, and revolved about a different one, cartwheeling.

I opened my eyes for one blink and regretted it. Colors I couldn't put a name to, and unearthly shapes that seemed to pass through my body. I started to vomit and choked it back.

"Don't look!" the bird shrieked, and I squeezed my eyes shut, hard, the acid taste burning my throat and soft palate, anxiety rising. "Only a few minutes more. Calm down."

Maybe this was hell, I thought. Maybe I did pull the trigger, and this was my punishment—not imps and flames, but an eternity of confusion and nausea.

It was shorter than eternity, though. Eventually the sensation subsided, and the bird told me to open my eyes.

Once more I had the sense of "being" the room, and then the raven materialized, and so did I. I sat down on the soft floor, exhausted.

"You've read *Mars as the Abode of Life*," it said, "by Percival Lowell."

"You know everything I read?"

"That, and more. You also read your namesake's book, of course."

"Have we . . . have you gone all the way to Mars?"

"No. Lowell was wrong. Mars never had anything more interesting than moss. But there are living creatures elsewhere."

"Venus?"

"You know what a Bessemer converter is."

I remembered the flame- and smoke-belching refineries of Pittsburgh. "Venus is like that?"

"Worse. No place in your solar system, other than Earth, has life that's at all interesting. There's some wildlife on satellites of Jupiter and Saturn, but they're less intelligent than a congressman, as Mark Twain would say. Dumber than a snail, actually.

"We've gone farther than that. Ten million times farther." The door opened and a soft reddish glow came in, like the end of sunset.

I stepped to the door. The sun was not setting; it was two hand spans above the horizon. There was enough mist or smoke in the air that I could look at it directly. It was much larger than our sun, and it looked like a piece of coal in a cooling stove, bright red with crusts of black.

Perhaps I *had* gone to hell. The landscape was Dantean, treeless chalk cliffs with precipitous overhangs. We stepped outside and were on such an overhang ourselves, facing a drop of a hundred yards down to a brown trickle of water. The air was hot and chalky, like a schoolroom in summer, after the boards are cleaned.

There was vegetation on our side of the gorge, weeds and gnarled bushes that were purple rather than green. They all stuck out of the cliff at the same angle, pointing toward the sun.

"The sun never moves," the raven said. "This planet always keeps one face to it, as often happens, given enough time."

"Like the moon, or Mercury," I said.

"Half right," he said. "They're wrong about Mercury."

He suddenly became old Gordon, and took my hand in his. "We're going to fly now. Don't be afraid."

"Fly?" Something pressed up under my feet and we rose, slowly at first, and floated out over the precipice. That set my heart to hammering, and I squeezed his hand so hard his knuckles cracked.

"There's no way you could drop. Relax and enjoy the view." We stopped rising and moved forward, faster and faster, with no wind or sense of acceleration.

(Gordon was still wearing only his hair, which came down far enough in back for a semblance of modesty. But only in back.)

On the other side of the canyon, the vegetation was sparse and regularly spaced, not in cultivated rows as such, but rather in that each commanded a certain area of ground, larger for the larger clumps and plants. Some seemed to be the size of trees, though it was hard to estimate, not really knowing how high we were. I studied the plants fiercely; it helped me fight the anxiety of flying.

"I wanted to stop here first partly because it so resembles your Christian concept of hell. But it's heaven to the people who live here."

"People?"

"Or 'creatures.' In Tlingit there's a word that encompasses both. There!"

We descended toward what looked like a patch of a different kind of vegetation, a clump of large transparent tubes. Unlike the other plants, though, they were mobile, twining slowly around each other. They looked like something that belonged in the sea, caressed by slow currents.

As we touched ground, he changed back into his avian manifestation. "They know me as Raven," he said, and I heard the capitalization. He fluttered down to the base of the seven tubes. "Take off your shoes."

I did, and the ground was surprisingly pleasant, warm and spongy. I worked my toes into it, though, and was rewarded by a sharp pinch.

"Don't do that. This is their brain you're standing on—the part they all share, anyhow. Stand still and they'll talk to you through your feet."

That's exactly what they did, and it was amazing. It felt as if they'd asked me a thousand questions over the course of a minute, and my brain responded directly, without translating the answers into speech.

They talked back, in a sense. It wasn't language so much as feeling. There was sympathy for my loss—six of them were children of the central one—but an admonition to hold on to life, although what they actually meant was both more specific and harder to express. The point of life was, to them, posing problems and solving them, and passing on the solutions.

"These people were old before life appeared on your Earth," Raven said. "This particular seven has been alive for more than a million years."

"Are they immortal? They'll live forever?"

"No. They'll live another million or ten million years. When they agree to die, they produce a spore, which will grow into another family on this spot."

"Another seven?"

"Or eleven, sometimes, or thirteen. One of them volunteers to stay alive for awhile and act as parent, as teacher.

"It's not suicide, since their essence is preserved in the parent, as is the essence of the thousand generations that went before."

How ugly and alien they might seem if I hadn't been literally in touch with them. Worms wriggling around, sticky secretions. But they were in a state of perfect love, angels living in hell. "Why do they have to die?"

"They die when they've learned all they can. You know of Mendel's genetics experiments."

"Yes." Again, it hadn't been a question.

"They need to replace themselves with a genetically different family. A group that can look at all the accumulated knowledge from a different point of view."

"That's all they do?" I said. "They don't have to worry about food, water, shelter?"

"Angels don't strive. They absorb radiant energy through the plants around them. They have a thing like a taproot that extends below the water table. As for shelter, there's no weather on this part of the planet—though it's fierce around the circumference where dark meets light, a never-ending storm."

"But if they don't go anyplace or do anything, how can they find new things to think about?"

"It comes to them through people like you and me. They've never met anyone from Earth before, so you gave them lots of new experiences and feelings to consider."

"You said they know you. You're from Earth."

"Not actually. I'm a kind of a visitor. A 'guardian' is the closest human word."

"My guardian?"

"Don't flatter yourself." He hopped around to face the angels. "People like me are especially interesting to them, because we travel around. They want to know where they themselves came from, and how and why they wound up here."

"Couldn't it be like Darwin contends? If they evolved from simpler forms, they wouldn't remember that far back, any more than we remember being infants."

"Very good, Rosa, but that's the point: on this whole planet there's nothing more complicated than a bush. Nothing for them to have evolved *from*.

"Furthermore, on almost every planet there's a particular kind of molecule that every living thing has. That's true of every other species here, but not of them: they have a different molecule."

"So they originally came from another planet?"

"That's the simplest explanation. But their curiosity is not just a matter of genealogy—they wonder whether they were put here for some purpose, and what it might be."

I smiled. "That sounds familiar."

He let out an annoyed squawk, and continued in Gordon's voice. "I'm not trafficking in religion here. These people don't even know whether they're natural, or some sort of artificially contrived biological machine, hidden in this out-of-the-way place to grind away at information for millions of millennia, ultimately to solve some problem that now is still beyond their ken.

"And if they *are* machines to that purpose, will they be switched off once they solve the problem?"

They began singing then. There was no other noise in this still place, except when Raven or I talked, but at first I didn't realize it was coming from them. It was a sweet pure sound, like a glass harmonica, complex chords that became words in English:

Before you go back to Earth
Before you go home
Come here to share what you've learned
Come here to learn what we've thought about you.

"That's unusual," Raven said. "I didn't know they could do that."

"Can I, may I tell them 'yes'?"

"Do."

I told them that I would be glad to help them in their quest, and their response was a jolt of pure sensual pleasure that started in the center of me and radiated out. I curled my toes into their brain and got the warning pinch again.

I didn't have a word for it then, orgasm, but I knew the feeling from Doc's tender ministrations. So the most powerful orgasm I'd ever had came through the soles of my feet, through the brain of seven man-sized worms. It was stranger than strange, but it did give me incentive to return.

"They know the workings of your body better than any human physicians could. I suspect they've fixed things here and there."

"They have." I moved my arm in a circle, and the shoulder pain was gone. So was the pain in my finger joints. "But I'm the first human being they've met! Human from Earth, I mean."

"They've seen a million varieties of both life and pain."

Including the pain of loss. I still grieved as strongly for Daniel, but it didn't make me want to stop living. I would live for both of us now.

"I could go back now," I said to Raven, "and be out of danger. God bless you for bringing me here."

"You might want to withhold your thanks for awhile." The golden room appeared behind him.

"That's right, other places to go." I tried to thank them with my most fervent prayer—praying through my feet!—then followed Raven into the room.

The cinnamon smell was gone, replaced by a soft musk, like the smell of a kitten. I closed my eyes and braced myself for the wrenching disorientation.

It wasn't as bad the second time. I knew what to expect, and knew it wouldn't last forever.

"Open your eyes." Room, raven, door. Outside the door, a steamy fetid jungle. "I'll go out first. They don't much like mammals here, except as food."

He hopped out into the jungle about twenty feet, looking left and right, and then began to change.

He grew to the size of an eagle, and then larger, impossibly large for a bird—and as he grew even larger, his shape changed, the wings becoming arms with taloned claws, his head a monstrous dragon's head. He yawned, showing rows of white fangs longer than fingers, and roared, as loud and deep as an ocean liner's foghorn. Steam issued from his horrible mouth; I expected flame.

The raven beckoned with impressive claws and I stepped out, a little apprehensive, feeling like food. But as soon as I was out of the room I started to transform, myself. My viewpoint rose higher off the ground and my vision began to change, as it had done when I was an eagle, eyes on opposite sides of my head.

I could feel my body bulking and changing. I leaned back naturally and balanced on a long thick tail. Tilting my head to inspect myself, I saw that I was a smaller version of the raven, with the same pebbly skin, but where he was glossy black, I was a kind of paisley of green and brown.

Ten or twelve feet tall, I probably weighed as much as a small elephant. And I had an elephant-sized hunger. Through the jungle smell of mold and earth, marigold and jasmine, came a clear note of rotting flesh, as mouth-watering to this body and brain as a pot roast to my other.

The raven made a series of grunts and clicks that I understood: "This way." He started crashing through the undergrowth and I followed him, rocking unsteadily from side to side at first, and then gaining confidence in the powerful legs.

We came to a clearing where a large creature, twice the size of the creature he had become, lay dead and quickly decomposing in the heat. About half had been eaten, perhaps by whoever killed it. Smaller lizards and things that seemed both lizard and bird were feasting on the carcass.

The raven roared at them, and I added my higher pitched scream. They backed and flapped away, not in total retreat, but just to wait while we had our fill.

"Hurry," the raven grunted and clicked. "Be ready to move fast."

I hesitated, not because the maggoty carcass looked unpalatable—it looked as good as a beef Wellington—but because I wasn't sure how to go about it. My arms were too short for the hands to reach my mouth.

The raven tilted down, his tail extended for balance, and tore at the flesh with his jaws. I did the same, and with an odd memory of bobbing for apples, quite enjoyed gulping down bushels of wormy flesh, crunching through bones to get to the putrid softness inside.

After about a minute of heavenly feasting, there was a piercing screech and Raven butted me hard to distract me from the banquet. Two creatures even twice *his* size were stalking toward us, teeth bared, unmistakably challenging us to defend our lunch.

Raven bounded away, and I followed him. We scrambled back down the path he'd torn a few minutes before, and when we came to the end of it, crashed determinedly through the solid jungle. I looked back, and the giants weren't pursuing.

He wasn't just running away, though; he had a definite direction. The jungle thinned and we splashed across a wide shallow river, out onto an endless savannah.

On the horizon was a single black mountain. He tilted his head at it and grunted one syllable: "There."

We loped easily through the grass. I was aware that we had no real enemies here; I probably could have killed a lesser creature, like a human, with my breath alone. But we saw no other living things, which was no surprise. Our progress was as subtle as a loco-motive's.

The grass thinned as we approached the moun-tain's slope. When it became a rocky incline, Raven stopped abruptly and turned back into a bird. I felt an odd churning inside, and became a woman again. My limbs ached pleasantly from the exercise, but I urgently needed both toothbrush and toilet.

"Here." Raven hopped over to some tufts of grass. "Chew this." I did, and it had a pleasant mild garlic flavor. Then I retreated behind a rocky outcrop, feel-ing a little silly for my modesty, and took my ease, then used smooth pebbles to clean up, Arab style.

I rearranged the strange clothing and returned to Raven. "Thank you. That was a fascinating experi-ence."

"A diversion," he said, "and a quick lunch. This mountain is what we came for. You just shat upon a living creature."

"What?"

"Don't worry; we birds do it all the time. And it didn't notice." He turned to look up the slope. "It doesn't know I exist, though I've shared its mind twice. Its essence."

"What is it called?"

"It doesn't have language, with no one else to talk to. I call it the Dark Man."

"Could I share its . . . essence, too?"

"That's why I brought you here. But I warn you it's disturbing."

"More so than being threatened by hungry dinosaurs?"

"Oh, quite. Being a dinosaur yourself, you knew they'd leave you be once you surrendered the food."

He was right; I hadn't been scared, just annoyed. "What is there to fear here?"

"It's not fear. Just knowledge of a special kind. Do you remember the time you first truly knew you were going to die?"

I thought. "Actually, no. I'm not sure."

"It was when you saw the Brady photographs of the ruins of Atlanta. You were ten."

The memory opened an emptiness. "All right. So this will be like that?"

"Perhaps worse. But I think you have to see it."

"Right here?"

"No. We have to fly to the top." He turned me

into the eagle again. "Don't think about what you're doing. Just look at where you want to go."

It was more complicated than that, but then suddenly simple, once I let instinct take over. I flapped awkwardly a number of times, but when I was a couple of yards off the ground, realized I should tilt into the warm wind that rose up the side of the mountain of the Dark Man. Then I could spiral up almost without effort.

A shadow passed over me and I looked up to see a flying lizard about my own size. Instead of a beak, it had a mouth like a barracuda's, fangs overlapping up and down. It opened the mouth and screeched, and after a moment of terror I realized it wasn't after me; it was threatening, warning me off the smaller prey. It dropped, talons out.

"Raven!" I cried.

Just before it reached him. Raven turned into a monstrous machine of articulated shiny metal, twice the lizard's size. The thing struck him with a clang; he slapped it off with a razor wing and it sped away in bleeding confusion.

Raven kept his metallic form until we reached the top. We both sculled onto a flat space and he turned back into a raven, and I into a woman.

"This way," he said, hopping toward a dark cave. I was annoyed that he didn't thank me for warning him about the danger. For a girl from Philadelphia, I made a pretty competent eagle.

At the entrance to the cave, he stopped, and turned into old Gordon. He said a few words in Tlingit.

"Ask its permission to enter."

"I thought you said the Dark Man wasn't aware of us."

"He isn't, himself, but his body has defenses. It took me awhile to figure this out: it won't admit any creature that doesn't have a language."

"Any language?"

"Just ask it permission."

The lines in bad Latin and French came to mind. "May I please come in, Dark Man?"

I guess I expected a magic door to creak open or something. But nothing changed, except for a slight cool breeze from the darkness. He changed back into a raven and hopped into the mouth of the cave, and I followed.

We picked our way through a jumbled pile of bones.

"You said it doesn't have a language. Yet it only admits people and things who do?"

"Strange, isn't it?" As if on cue, the huge toothy

flying reptile skidded to a halt a few feet away, outside the cave mouth. Raven shrieked a warning at it, a painfully loud scream that reverberated in the small space. But the lizard had seen us change back into something resembling food, and of course didn't stop to consider the oddness of that. It hopped into the cave, baring teeth, and approached the pile of bones, leathery wings dragging behind, leaving a smear of blood.

It couldn't see us. "Maybe you better change back," I whispered.

Hearing me, it tilted its head to peer into the darkness. It picked up a long bone in a taloned foot and delicately gnawed on one end. Then it dropped it and raised its wings in a kind of protective tent over its head and made a sound between a growl and a crow's caw, and stalked toward us over the bones, all teeth and terrible purpose. It got about halfway— I looked to Raven, who was watching with calm curiosity—and it suddenly stopped, cried out, and pitched forward, obviously dead.

"What happened?"

"I don't know. Want to do an autopsy?"

"But . . . how did *you* know? This is his planet, and he just walked in and died."

"It's his planet, but there's only one Dark Man on

it. Creatures who find their way into the cave just die; they don't have any way to warn the next creature. Unless they have language, in which case there's no danger."

"But how did you find that out?"

"I'm always asking around. Someone on another planet told me about the Dark Man and I came here. It's an interesting experience."

"Disturbing, you said."

"That, too. Can you see me well enough to follow?"

He was black against gray. "Go ahead."

It was less scary than a cave on Earth. Cool and damp, but nothing like spiders or bats—unless they could talk, I supposed. As we moved farther in, slightly uphill, it was obvious that the walls were dimly phosphorescent. We went around a curve and there was no more light from the entrance behind us, but I could still see Raven, and rocks along the path.

We went around another bend and there was a faint flickering light. Then a steep incline, perhaps fifty yards, and we entered the large chamber from which the light was coming.

It was a window to the sky. But it wasn't obviously sky—it was a bluish-gray vista, on which concentric circular lines of light were superimposed, flickering.

"The circles are stars," Raven said. "Months are going by every second. This window faces what would be north, in Alaska, so we see the circumpolar stars rotating around the pole. But they're going so fast they look like streaks." He hopped up a pile of rocks that formed a natural staircase, and I followed with ease.

Below us spread the broad savannah and the thick jungle, separated by the river. The jungle seemed to vibrate, as trees died and were replaced. The river itself undulated, coiling like a slow serpent.

"It must take centuries for a river to change its course like that," I said. Raven nodded like a human, staring.

Over the space of a few seconds, the savannah was transformed into pastureland. Huts of wood and stone—pieces of the Dark Man?—appeared and disappeared.

Parts of the jungle were cleared and a bridge snapped into place over the river. A town appeared and became a city, with regular streets and tall buildings on both sides of the river. Two more bridges appeared. The city spread out to the horizon, and it seemed almost to be dancing, as new buildings replaced old ones in ripples of progress.

A throbbing curve of fire on the horizon. "That's a spaceport," Raven said, "where they leave for other stars. They won't get to Earth; it's too far away. And they don't have much time."

As he said that, there was a lurch, and the city was suddenly leveled, a static jumble of ruins. The river started to move again, and widened into a lake.

In less than a minute, the jungle reclaimed the ruins on the other side of the water.

"Look at the stars," the raven said.

"I don't see anything different."

"Keep looking. Use that hill on the horizon as a reference."

I looked at the hill for a minute and saw that the circles of stars were slowly crawling to my right.

"What's happening?"

"The Dark Man is turning around to face the sun. The land nearby is moving with him."

"Is that what happened to the city—was it an earthquake when the Dark Man started to move?"

"No. They did that to themselves. Happens."

"People appeared and disappeared just like that?"

"It was actually quite a long time, to them. And they weren't people as such—as I said, mammals are just food here. They were lizards similar to the ones in the jungle—much like you were, but with longer arms and useful hands."

I remembered how it felt. "Just as vicious, though."

"Something they had in common with humans."

I looked out over the expanse, now apparently an inland sea. There was no sign of their civilization.

"The Dark Man has seen this happen before, and it may happen again. He's turning around to watch the sun because it changes on a time scale that's meaningful to him. He'll watch it die, over billions of years."

"Does this always happen?"

"Stars dying? Of course."

"No—I mean the lizards. Does civilization always bring ruin?"

"Not always. Often."

He hopped down the steps to lead me back down the corridor. "It's all timing. Once a species learns how to exchange ideas, a process is set in motion that might ultimately result in permanent peace and harmony. But it's not inevitable."

"As in our case. Humans."

"Timing, as I say. In one way of looking at it, humans discovered fire a little too early; fire and metals. From there on, it's only a matter of time before a species learns to use the forces that make stars burn. If they haven't grown past the need to wage war by then, their prospects aren't good."

I stepped carefully down the wet rocks, thinking of how I had saved my son from a senseless war, only to have him killed by a senseless man. "So you say that humanity is going to go the way of these lizards."

"You're asking me to predict the future, which is meaningless. There are many futures." He started down the corridor. "Come on. More places to see."

On the last step, I twisted my ankle and fell. He hopped back when he heard me cry out, changing into old Gordon, who gave me a hand.

We hobbled along. "It's only a couple of hundred yards to my ship. The room."

"It seems to go anywhere you want," I said through clenched teeth. "Why not just whistle for it?"

"It can't come in here. Time is funny in here, as you may have noticed."

We came out of the cave into a pelting rain. He carried me the few steps to the yellow light. Once inside, my ankle immediately stopped hurting. The place, or thing, smelled like cinnamon again.

"You should open up a clinic," I said. He'd changed back into a raven. "You'd be the richest bird on Earth."

"I already am, when I'm on Earth."

"You travel like this, most of the time?"

"Time, space." He flexed his wings in an unmistakable shrug. "I do keep moving, observing. But in a way, I'm always in Sitka. Gordon doesn't disappear for months at a time. "

"I don't understand."

"You will. Soon." We both dissolved into the now-familiar transition state.

A moment later, we were back in the yellow room. "Did something go wrong?"

"No," he said. "We're never far from this place."

The door opened and I stepped toward it. "Don't go outside. Just look. I think if we went outside we couldn't get back in."

"Where are we?" It looked like a quiet woodland.

"There isn't any 'where' or 'when' here. Everybody sees something different. Tell me what you think it is."

I stepped cautiously to the door. There was a disturbing noise.

It was a quiet woodland otherwise. Birds twittering. The smell of green growing things. Buds flowering.

A pear tree with a single large fruit. A snake the size of a python draped among its limbs.

"The Garden of Eden?" I said. "This can't be real."

"Whatever it is or is not, it's real. Do you see the pain yet?"

The room moved over a thick stand of bushes, toward the noise. "Stay inside," Raven repeated.

In a small clearing, a pregnant woman lay on her back. She was covered with streaks of blood, hair matted with it. She was grunting and whimpering hoarsely with exhaustion and pain. God, had I ever been there. I took an instinctive step forward.

Gordon suddenly appeared, blocking the door. "Stay. I mean it. There's nothing you can do."

"All right," I said. He turned around and looked out the door.

The woman—I couldn't think of her as "Eve"—was very close to giving birth. Her womb was dilating and I could see the top of the head, hair black as her own.

Blood oozed around the presenting head. Her body writhed and she screamed, keening.

"Steady," Gordon said, a hand on my shoulder.

"I've seen this before," I said. "I've done it."

"Not like this, I think."

Her womb opened impossibly wide and for a moment the screaming stopped—then in a spray of blood the head came out It was an adult's head.

Her own head? Now *it* started screaming; even

louder. With a start, I saw that the mother's head and neck had disappeared.

Her womb split horribly sideways, and a bloody shoulder worked its way out. She was giving birth to herself, turning inside out.

The screams stopped only long enough for her to take deep ragged breaths. The other shoulder worked through, distorting the mother's torso into something made of human parts but not recognizably human.

Both breasts slid out at once—and it became horrifyingly clear that the self she was giving birth to was also pregnant.

I didn't know the word then, but she was everting herself. The body split and after the abdomen worked its way through, the rest was swift: the new womb and then her limbs and feet. All streaked with bright fresh blood.

The newborn mother began to whimper and clutch at the bloodied grass.

"Oh, my God. She's starting over."

"You see a woman." He was Raven again.

"You don't?"

"I almost did, as Gordon. Now what I see is the Orion Nebula: the dying and birthing of stars. It goes on all the time, of course."

"But this *pain*."

"You think the universe feels nothing, giving birth and dying? Any pain you've ever felt was only an echo of that."

I watched with horrified fascination as the process started over. "That's only metaphor," I said. "The universe doesn't have flesh and ganglia and a brain to interpret their distress signals."

"Why do you think you have them? One of your own said 'Pain is nature's way of telling us we're alive.' That's close to literal truth."

I was obstinate. "Pain draws our attention to something being wrong with the body."

"What did I just say? Your body was perfectly happy when it was a scattered bunch of oxygen and hydrogen and carbon atoms. Life *is* what's wrong with it."

"Now that's a wonderful argument against suicide. When I die, the universe will be a smidgeon happier."

"This is not an argument. I'm just showing you around. What you do when we return to Sitka . . . will be what you do."

"Including . . . take my life?"

"Life was yours to give and it's yours to take. But I don't think you will kill yourself now. Let's go to one more place; then we'll start back." I shut my eyes hard and endured the whirling dislocation. It went longer than ever before, and I clenched my jaws so hard against being sick that I could hear my teeth grinding. Finally it was over.

"This is not a world," he said as I opened my eyes, "in the sense of being a planet. It's not even really a place, as your Garden of Eden was not an actual woodland." The door opened. "But I think we'll both see the same thing this time."

I stepped to the opening and took hold of the edge of the door. We were evidently floating over a landscape, drifting a few hundred yards off the ground. Dramatic mountains and cliffs, but not menacing like the first planet. Everything was subtle shades of warm gray, soft and monochromatic.

There was no horizon. The landscape stretched out forever, becoming vague with distance.

"Let's go on down," Raven said.

As we floated closer to the ground, what had appeared to be a kind of granular texture became thousands of individuals, perhaps millions.

Some few were human beings, but the overwhelming majority were otherworldly creatures. Gargoyles and sprites. Demons and floating jellyfish, an articulated metal spider and a close formation of thousands of blue bees arranged in a perfect cube. Two dinosaurs like we had been and a cluster of six of the translucent angel creatures we saw on the first planet.

"Only six?" I said.

The raven bobbed his head. "The six who elected to die."

"Wait . . . everyone here is dead? This is the afterlife?"

"They're not completely dead. But they're not really alive, in the sense of eating and breathing—if they were eating, a lot of them would eat each other; if they were breathing, they'd be breathing different atmospheres, usually poisonous to the others."

"Daniel! Is Daniel here?"

"He might be someplace. I wouldn't know where to find him, though. And you couldn't talk to him or touch him.

"I really don't understand this place, the where and how of it. The 'why' seems to be that it's a holding area of some kind."

"Of souls," I said. "After they die."

"They look like bodies to me."

"Waiting for something?"

"I don't know. If it's something like your Catholics'

purgatory, then I wonder where heaven is. I've never come across it."

"Maybe your room, your ship, can't get there. Maybe you do have to die and spend some time here, first."

"Your guess is as good as mine. Almost as good, anyhow."

There didn't seem to be much order in the crowd. I tried to pick out the humans, and the nearly human, and there did seem to be a lot of the very old and the very young, as you would expect of the dead. Nobody really *looked* dead, though. No wounds or signs of disease.

But nobody was moving. It was like a photograph in three dimensions. While I was looking, two new ones appeared, one like a human woman but with spadelike appendages instead of hands, the other a kind of long-haired monkey with an extra pair of legs.

"Does everybody come here, good or bad?"

"Impossible to say. There appears to be room for about everybody." We started to rise at an accelerating rate. The individuals merged back into the granular texture and then into a smooth gray; mountains shrank to pebbles and themselves disappeared. The horizon didn't change, though.

"What happens if you fly in one direction for a long time?"

"It doesn't seem to change. You never come to an edge. But 'a long time' doesn't mean much here. The illusion of time belongs to worlds like yours. Here, there's only will and chance."

"What do you mean by that? Time an illusion?"

"When you studied mathematics, you used the idea of infinity."

"Of course. You couldn't do calculus without it."

"And you believe the universe is infinite." I nodded. "So stars and planets and nebulae go on forever."

"Of course."

"Well, I have news for you: they don't. Within your lifetime, scientists will suspect that there's an edge to it. Within another lifetime, they'll prove there is."

"That's curious. So what's beyond it?"

"Another universe. And another and another. Every instant, from the universe's birth to its death, exists side by side, in a way. Think of it as an Edison cinematograph, writ very large: one frozen moment, then the next, and so on.

"Furthermore, every possible universe exists as well. Many where the Civil War didn't happen or was won by the South. Many where you did kill yourself Thursday evening. Many where you had biscuits for breakfast, instead of toast. With everything else in the universe unchanged. There's room for them all.

"What you perceive as time is your translation from one possible moment to the next, because of something you did or something the universe did to you."

"Free will and predestination?" I said.

"Decision and chance," the raven said, "inextricably intertwined."

We had risen so high that a featureless gray plane faded off into mist. Above the mist, blackness, no stars.

"But this place, this is beyond that?"

"Yes. This is where people go when they stop moving from moment to moment."

"So maybe this *is* heaven?"

He just looked at me. "Close your eyes. We're going back to the angels."

I didn't close my eyes, at first—after all, while we were traveling, I didn't seem to exist as an assemblage of body parts, so what did "closed eyes" mean? In a few seconds it became pretty obvious, if not describable. Like seasickness, but somehow larger, longer, with the threat that it could last forever. I did something like closing eyes and the room disappeared, and I only felt miserable. The smell of musk changed to lemon.

Then it was cinnamon and we were there, on the

Dantean planet. Through the open door, the seven angels braided together in the oven heat. "Let me speak to them first," Raven said. He hopped over to the dark soft patch he called their brain.

They were momentarily still, rigid, and then resumed a rhythmic twining. "Now you," he said. "Shoes off."

The ground was like hot flour between my toes. But I remembered not to dig in when I stepped onto their coolness.

At first I didn't hear or feel anything. Then there was something like a quiet song, a wordless hymn in my mind. I concentrated, but couldn't make any sense of it. Then it was gone.

"Won't you use words?" I said. But they just curled and uncurled in silence.

The raven was back in the yellow room. "I think they're done. Come on."

I crossed the hot sand, looking back at them. "Did they tell you anything?"

"Nothing I didn't already know. They like you."

I couldn't take my eyes off them, as I backed into the cube. "Then why didn't they say anything?" It smelled of mint tea.

"They don't so much say things as do things." The yellow wall appeared. "Close your eyes."

This time I obeyed. "Are we going back?"

"Yes and no." I squeezed my eyes shut. The dislocation seemed about as long as the first one.

"You can look now." The door was open on a scene of incredible desolation, stone buildings battered to rubble, a few steel skeletons standing. Everything blackened by fire.

"Where is this?"

"Times Square, New York City." He had turned into Gordon, who blinked away tears. I had never seen him cry. "Your world, about a hundred years after you were born."

"Like . . . like the lizards' world?"

"Exactly. No human left alive." He turned to me with a kind of smile. "I feel like the Ghost of Christmas Yet to Come. This is what usually happens. Not always in the middle of the twentieth century. Sometimes it takes another hundred or even a thousand years."

"But it always happens."

"Not always." He changed back into Raven. "You don't want to go outside here. You would die. Close your eyes."

"Where are we going?"

He didn't reply, but I felt weight on my body, the compression of stays around my waist, and took one quick look. Instead of the strange skintight suit, I was wearing my warm-weather teaching clothes, the light gray Gibson Girl suit I'd mail-ordered from San Francisco.

I screwed my eyes shut again, against the rush of nausea. "We're going back to Sitka?"

"Yes."

"I'll freeze to death in this!"

"You'll manage."

The machine stopped. I felt a breath of cool forest air and heard crickets.

We were back in the woods where we'd started. But there was no snow. The light of a full moon filtered through the forest canopy. An owl called and flapped away. I stepped out onto soft humus and the yellow room disappeared behind me.

"Months have passed," I said. "It must be June or July." I slapped a mosquito.

Raven beat the air with his wings and rose to an eye-level branch. "Something has passed."

I had a chill that had nothing to do with temperature. "You said you were a guardian, but not my guardian. Are you going off to save someone else now?"

"I think I'm done here. I don't save lives. I save life. By making the smallest change I can."

"Life?"

"Think about what I've said." He hopped around in a full circle, the moonlight glinting soft rainbows off his feathers. Then he cawed, like an actual raven, and flew off into the night

"Wait!" I said, but he was above the trees and soaring.

For a moment I was totally lost, and started to panic, but got ahold of myself. Sitka *was* an island, after all; if I walked in any direction I'd eventually come to the water, and there take my bearings.

Bears. I whistled, the way Gordon had taught me. Raven. They won't attack you if you don't surprise them. Unlike some other mammals.

I could have gone in any direction, but made the assumption that Raven's room, or ship, had come down in the same place from which it had left, in the same orientation. I picked my way through the undergrowth in a straight line for a few minutes, and was rewarded with a game trail. I turned left and walked down the hill.

I thought I knew where I was, but the place where my cabin should have been was just a small clearing. In a few more steps, though, I was on the path that turned into Lincoln Street.

The moon was high, but somewhat west. It was

probably about two in the morning. The town was quiet except for faint noise drifting up from the harbor.

I came to a slight rise and looked down in that direction. There were work lights arranged around one of the boats, which looked vaguely familiar.

A chill gripped me. It was the *White Nights,* and the noise was from a work crew belowdecks, banging rivets into the boiler.

I broke into a run, as fast as my skirts would allow! I ran downhill to Baranoff Street, paused to get my breath, and walked swiftly to the Baranoff Hotel.

There was a light on in the lobby. I rushed up the steps, but the door was locked. When I tapped on the glass, the little old lady came 'round, thumb holding her place in a dime novel.

She unlocked the door and a hundred wrinkles pinched into a frown. "What on earth are you doing about at this hour?"

"I couldn't sleep," I improvised, "and went down to check on the ship."

She looked at the key in her hand, evidently trying to remember having let me out. "Down to the docks after midnight," she clucked. "You're daft. But ye must have a guardian angel."

"Yes!"

I rushed by her and up the stairs to the room that Daniel and I had shared. The door was locked, I tapped, and then knocked loudly.

He opened the door and stood there bleary-eyed, completely alive. I grabbed him and hugged him so hard his joints popped. "My son . . . do I have a story to tell you."

The incredible tale.

With the spirit-lamp I made us some tea, trying not to talk too fast. He became more and more alert.

After about ten minutes, after I'd left him and Doc and Chuck in Skagway and come back to Sitka and teaching, he said, "Wait. What about Soapy Smith and his gang?"

"What about him? He was killed in a shoot-out before we came to Sitka."

"You really think that?"

"I remember it clearly. Reverend Bower told me about it before we left. And then I read about it in the Skagway *News,* too; about the man who killed him later dying in the hospital."

Daniel shook his head. "Mother . . . Soapy Smith isn't dead. Not yet, though they'll hang him for sure."

"Isn't dead?"

"No. There was some sort of town meeting about what to do with him, and he and his gang went to break it up, and it turned into a massacre. Then a lot of the town joined in, one side or the other, and there was a lot of shooting, all through the night. By noon the next day, the army had come down from Dyea and shut down the town. It's under martial law—you don't remember any of this?"

"No." It was a different world.

"Mother, we talked all afternoon about it! Whether or not to go on!" Hysteria edging into his voice.

"And . . . what did we decide?"

"We didn't. Me and Chuck want to go on, at least to Juneau, and wait and see. You and Doc, you wanted to chuck it, sell the gear and go back to the States."

It was sinking in. I had a funny thought. "So Chuck wants to dock it, and Doc wants to chuck it."

He nodded rapidly, smiling with relief. "That's what you said over dinner. Is it coming back to you?"

I thought about Raven's cinematographs—millions of them clicking along in unison; one frame changing, and then another.

"Where did this dress come from?"

"What?"

"I distinctly remember buying this dress by mail order from a discount house in San Francisco, five or six weeks after you left for the Yukon."

"Mother, I—"

"Of course you don't keep track of your mother's wardrobe. But do you ever remember me wearing anything but black since we left Kansas?"

He picked up his tea and then silently set it down. He stepped over to the bureau and brought back a bottle, and poured an inch of whiskey into the cup. He stirred it with his finger and took a reflective sip.

"No. All your clothes are black. And there's no place you could have bought that tonight, after we went to bed."

That amused me as much as it annoyed me. "Daniel! You think I would go out and buy a new suit just to back up some crazy story?"

He cringed a little. "But it *is* a crazy story."

"I suppose it is." I poured a tablespoon of the liquor into my own tea. "And it gets much crazier."

I condensed my teaching and missionary work to

about a minute, and then spent another minute explaining the role of the Raven in the Tlingit religion.

"What's so important about this raven?"

I told him about his death and my reaction. He shook his head, openmouthed.

"I was . . . going to kill myself, and then a raven appeared. Just as I cocked the gun. He walked through the door as if it weren't there, and said, 'God wouldn't want you to do that.' Or something to that effect."

"A magic bird talked to you."

"Indeed. And then he changed *me* into a bird. An eagle."

"Mother . . ."

"Just hear me out. I know this sounds like madness—maybe I *am* mad! But if I don't tell someone, I'll burst."

"Go ahead." His mouth was trembling, his eyes wide.

I hesitated. Could I tell him about Eve birthing herself, about my transformation into a ravenous reptile, about being the Dark Man and watching a world's birth, growth, and death?

"Do you remember Flammarion's *Lumen*?" He shook his head. "It's the book I read on the Mississippi, that the two French girls loaned to me."

"Oh, yes," he said, visibly relieved. "They were cute."

"The hero of that book, Lumen, has a sort of spirit guide, Quaerens, who takes him out into space and shows him . . . something of the nature of the universe. That's what happened to me."

The mantle on the kerosene lamp started to sputter. Daniel lit a candle and turned off the lamp. Our shadows wavered and loomed like watching ghosts.

"So this bird was your spirit guide?"

"He took the form of a raven because it was convenient and appropriate. What he showed me, though . . ." I sipped the cooling tea and gathered my thoughts.

"He showed me that every world that is possible does exist somewhere. I couldn't live in the world where you and Doc had died in a senseless tragedy. When I tried to take myself from that world with the Pinkerton man's revolver—"

"We pawned that revolver in Seattle."

"In *this* world! In mine, I talked you into leaving it with me, and so in Dawson City you faced a gunman unarmed, and died. And when I tried to use it to leave that world, Raven—the raven appeared."

"And he guided you here."

"Somehow." I took his hand in both of mine and stopped holding back tears. "Somehow."

He gently extricated himself and began pacing.

"And this also happened to the Lumen guy in the book?"

I thought for a moment, wiping my eyes. "No . . . not to him personally. He just observed it."

He leaned on the windowsill and looked out. The sky was just starting to lighten into peach; short summer nights. "It could have been a dream."

"No."

Still talking to the window: "Watching the crewman die so horribly—that did happen in your world?"

"It did."

"Well, it gave *me* nightmares. Probably will for the rest of my life. Maybe—"

"It gave *me* nightmares, too—more than half a year ago!"

He turned and gave me a weary and troubled look.

"All right," I said, "If I've been in Sitka for only a day, where and how did I learn Tlingit? *Kit-ka'ositiya-ga-yet.*"

Hearing me say those alien syllables—it had taken me months before I could say them without the children hiding their smiles behind hands—that was probably more solid proof than the clothing that wasn't black.

"What does that mean?" He came back and sat across from me.

"It's Raven's original name. What else would you like me to say?"

He shook his head. "What happens . . . happened in Dawson City?"

"Some drunkard picked a fight with Doc. You went to help him and the man pulled out a gun and shot both of you, heart and head."

"How did you hear about it?"

"Chuck dictated a letter. The man who wrote it, Morris Chambers, said you were very brave. Doc was, too." I made a helpless gesture. "I wish I could show it to you. But I have nothing from that world except my memories, and what I'm wearing."

"You don't need anything. Mother." He kneaded his forehead. "I have to believe you. Even if that world was some kind of dream, it was also real."

"Or this world is the dream, as it seems to me. Maybe they're all dreams, in the mind of God."

He almost said something about that, but kept his peace. From my distant perspective now, I can see that I'd just put another piece of fuel on his smoldering atheism. He'd witnessed the most horrible death he would see in his whole lifetime, and then his mother wakes him up in the middle of the night with the strangest tale he would ever hear.

If there is a God, he would say in later life, He's not the sort of person I'd want over for dinner.

"Are you going to tell Chuck and Doc?"

I thought for a moment. "What do you think?"

"I don't know. Doc would believe you if you told him black was white."

I smiled. "Chuck is not so smitten."

"Chuck's down-to-earth."

So was I, finally, gladly. "For now, let's keep it between you and me." He nodded vigorously. I stood and picked up the candle. "Now you try to get some sleep. I have to write for awhile."

The room had a small table with a straight-backed chair. I picked up my diary. The last entry was about the horrific accident with the boiler, with a few lines about Sitka. I hadn't gone to meet Reverend Bower.

In this world, I never would, I thought.

I wrote as fast as the words would come. Daniel tossed and turned, silently got up and had another drink, and finally snored.

First I described the worlds Raven had shown me, a sketchy account that I would later expand, and the sun was bright and high by the time I got to my return to Earth and Raven's odd statement. Guardian, not of my life, but of life itself.

The world reborn.

There was a soft knocking on the door. I opened it a crack and saw Doc. "Dan's still asleep," I whispered.

"Chuck, too," he said. "Hard night for them both. You want breakfast?"

I slipped out into the hall and resisted the impulse to hug him and smother him with kisses. He had not known me for nearly as long as I'd known him.

"Nice dress," he said. "Don't recall it."

Downstairs, I smelled ham frying, and my stomach growled almost as loudly as the dinosaur it had inhabited the last time I ate. That amused Doc, and I was able to resist the impulse to explain.

The meal was the first experience of a kind of sensory double vision that would haunt me for the next half-century. The ham and eggs and fried bread were delicious and filling. But they were nothing compared to tearing into the putrid flesh of a well-aged reptile. Never again in my life would I eat that simply and that well. (Perhaps because I would never again *be* that simple and healthy.)

Over breakfast I had to be a little calculating. Doc was infatuated with me—in his world, we'd made love only a few days before, in a way that was pretty serious in 1898. He was a very nice man, but he *was* a man, and I was an object of both love and lust.

I had a week's more knowledge of him than he had of me, but my memory of that week was a half-year old, and rather a lot had happened between then and now. I also had a memory of a yesterday that didn't quite happen here, and I couldn't be sure what was different, besides the fate of a Skagway gangster and his cronies. Who was president? Did they know Mars had moons?

I knew Mercury didn't keep one face always to the sun. Should I tell anybody?

The breakfast was good. Doc was almost as hungry as I was, and we said little until the plates were cleared and we went to the parlor for coffee.

"Rosa," he said in a conspiratorial tone, "I've been thinking about what you said yesterday." Not exactly what I wanted to hear. "Do you still feel the same way?" He touched my hand.

"Yes," I said, with what I hoped was the right amount of force. Was it marriage or a loan or the weather?

"Even if we could just break even, selling the kit, we'd have a solid two thousand dollars. Look at this." He took from his pocket a page of newsprint that had been folded into a small square, and carefully unfolded it.

It was a page of real estate advertisements from the paper we'd bought in San Francisco. Doc had penciled boxes around a few of the small farm notices.

What had I suggested? That we marry and become a farm family in California? Better than raising dust in Dodge, I supposed. But me a farm wife?

"Most of these got to be small farmers who took gold fever. If they still own the farm, it has to be producing better than most." The 1893–97 depression had hurt small farms across the country. Banks would foreclose and consolidate acreage to sell to absentee landlords or the large-scale "bonanza" farms.

From the perspective of a half-century later, I can see that buying a small farm and hoping to make a living from it was a quixotic fantasy—competing with large-scale farms that used cheap immigrant labor or, by the 1890s, huge machines for planting and cultivating.

But I didn't know that then. The idea of settling down in a peaceful country place was pretty compelling after the tumult that started when the Pinkerton man knocked on our door. Not to mention a whirlwind tour of the universe.

I studied the ads. "Most of these are orange groves. You've never raised citrus, have you?"

"No, but we had forty acres in fruit trees. Can't be all that different."

"But Chuck's against it."

"Not against us gettin' married." So that *was* the deal. "But him and Dan have this notion that they could still go on to the Yukon. Sell off some of the goods, so that you and me could go back to the States."

I shook my head. "Even with half the worth of the goods, we wouldn't have nearly enough money for any of these." I set the page down.

"That's true," he said, "but we could save up the

balance. I could hire myself out to any farm and you could teach or work for a business."

I was about to tell him how long it would take a teacher to save two thousand dollars, when a bell like a triangle rang urgently in the dining room. We got up and went to see what was happening.

It was the captain of the *White Nights* and his mate. The captain spoke stentorian Russian, one sentence at a time, and the mate translated in a normal tone of voice.

"This is for the people standing here who are passengers of the vessel *White Nights*. By telegraph we heard from Skagway an hour ago, about.

"No one is docking in Skagway until after the military says so. It is, what they say, a 'nobody in, nobody out' situation, while they make the tribunal. Two weeks more.

"We can not wait. The boiler is fix; we have funeral at noon and then steam out. We have to be back in Seattle nine days from hence.

"We can leave you and your cargos at Juneau or Fort Wrangell, or you can come back to Seattle with us at no charge. Or you can stay here. But we steam at two o'clock this afternoon." The captain jammed his hat on his head and stomped out, followed by the mate.

There was a moment of silence while the whole dining room, including Dan and Chuck, on the stairs in their nightclothes, watched the two men exit. Then seven or eight loud conversations started simultaneously. We motioned our sons to follow us into the parlor.

"Has to be Juneau," Daniel said, and Chuck nodded agreement.

"You don't want to stay there for two weeks," I said. "The noise would drive you mad." They gave me two quite different looks. "Or so I've read," I added. "We'll see when we get there."

We spent a few hours walking around Sitka. I kept my eyes open for things that might be different, but I hadn't been especially observant before. Doc was fascinated by the octagonal concrete building where, now, I would not be working for the next half-year.

Gordon was nowhere to be seen. There were lots of ravens, of course, but none of them seemed to pay us any special attention.

I had an impulse to wait around until ten, when the students would be coming in for the riot of summer arts and crafts work, to mentally say good-bye to them.

Suddenly I remembered the letter from Grace Loden in Fort Wrangell. I checked my purse and it was there. Doc chided himself for not reminding me about it—but we were both excused because of the horror and chaos of the boiler disaster.

We went inside and found Reverend Bower watering his flowers—but there the similarity to my old world ended. He did have the stock of old McGuffey readers, and some paper and pencils—but they had to be aboard in a couple of hours. Doc went off to hire a cart while Bower and I and the librarian boxed up the books and supplies.

He mentioned the job opening, and I regretfully turned him down.

Doc came back with a mule and cart he'd borrowed for six bits. Bower reimbursed him out of a petty cash box.

The boys were already on deck, and helped us add the school materials to our load. The boxes gave us a good solid wall for our makeshift tent. I thought about the ferocious storm, last time, and realized that we'd just miss it, if the weather in this world was the same.

A few minutes before two, the first mate walked around the deck wordlessly, checking off a list. Then he shouted something down to the dock and returned to the helm. The whistle shrieked and we were off.

We watched the icebergs at the Icy Strait again—

this time the crew palpably happy, knowing they wouldn't have to come back and hack them into blocks for ballast. The sky was pure cerulean blue, and a strong cool south wind pushed us along.

I was at the bow-rail with my hair undone, letting the breeze blow through it, when Daniel came to lean on the rail beside me. "So what is Juneau like?" he said quietly.

"Steep and loud. The town is built on the side of a hill. The noise from the rock-crushing machines across the bay is intolerable.

"The streets were rivers of mud, but we'd just had a heavy rain. I suspect they're pretty muddy all the time. A lot of the men carry guns, I guess because they're also carrying gold.

"Doc and I will go up the main street to a parlor where they have an Edison Spring Motor Phonograph. We'll listen to Scott Joplin on a new kind of cylinder. Brown wax."

He shook his head. "You really think Chuck and I won't be able to tolerate it?"

"I can't tell the future, son. Only the past."

"And it changes."

I nodded. "Like Soapy Smith and that little war they had, in this world. God only knows what effect that will eventually have."

"Or maybe God doesn't know anything. Or care." Chuck shouted for him and he left me with that.

What *was* God's place in this universe crammed with all possibilities? Was He a guide, or just an overseer?

Or was He just a fiction we made up to help us tolerate life, with all its random twists and turns, with all its unexplainable loss and pain?

Maybe that was something even Raven didn't know. Or he knew, and was cruel enough or kind enough not to tell me. We all wind up in that horizonless place when we stop moving from moment to moment. Perhaps whether we find it heaven or hell or purgatory depends on the choices we made along the way.

Perhaps it's just a graveyard.

It was just starting to get dark when we could hear the faint noise that would be such a din in Juneau. I realized that my prediction about the parlor with the phonograph was probably not going to come true—we wouldn't be in until late at night, and of course the place wouldn't be open.

The noise was plenty loud when Juneau was just a glow on the horizon. We had a family meeting and the boys agreed that Fort Wrangell would be a quieter place to wait out the news from Skagway.

By the time the port came into view, everybody had their ears plugged with something, or were trying to sleep under muffling pillows and piles of clothing. The first mate came around with his list, waking people up with the toe of his boot, asking whether people wanted to unload their kits here, or go on.

Only a handful had the combination of deafness and determination to face the prospect of weeks in that pandemonium. For the rest of us, the mate said we could go ashore and try to find someplace quieter, but if we weren't on board by nine A.M. sharp, they would steam without us.

Doc and I left the boys in a tavern loud enough to drown out the noise, and toiled uphill. On his own, I knew he would have stayed with them, but it was obviously no place for a woman.

We found the little café, and it was still open. The tinkling of Scott Joplin greeted our ears when Doc opened the door, and he brightened considerably when he saw two men drinking beer and whiskey.

The toothless round man was kindly a third time, the first for Doc, of course. At this late hour, he offered sliced sausage and cheese, rather than his wife's pastries.

We got our beer and coffee and sat apart from the

others. After two cylinders of Joplin, and on his second beer. Doc began the same outpouring I'd heard in the previous Juneau—memories of Lilian; love and loss.

It was different, though; more sentimental. Could it have been that this time he wasn't driven by a premonition of death? He faced an uncertain future again, but it was the kind of life he'd dealt with before. Perhaps he wanted me to know what I was getting into.

Around midnight I had a hot whiskey myself, to help me sleep through the noise, and we went on back to the ship. On the wharf there was a man standing on a box selling wax earplugs; we tried them, and found they were a quarter well spent.

The boys weren't back yet, unsurprisingly. Doc shouted that he would go search for them if they weren't back by daylight. We wrapped up in blankets and lay down together, hands touching.

I slept straight through until the whistle shrieked, ten minutes before casting off. Dan and Chuck were collapsed in their usual places, so I dozed for another hour or so, and then pried the stoppers out of my ears and made a breakfast of crackers and hard cheese.

The sky was threatening, so I started to set up our

area for the heavy storm I expected to hit before noon. The men woke up and helped me batten down the hatches.

Our sons were very much the worse for wear, and although I pitied them, I secretly hoped that a few hours of seasickness would be a salutary lesson.

The storm that hit was so violent that the lesson was probably lost, the sober and drunk clinging to the rail together. After an hour or so, my own stomach gave up the fight and started heaving, all four of us united in freezing misery.

It was the same storm as before, but this time we were headed into it, and the ship had the same violent rise and fall—up slow, down fast—that had made Dan and me so deathly ill on Lake Huron when we were fleeing Philadelphia.

The storm lasted all day, until sunset, which was about nine o'clock. As night fell, so did we, drenched and aching. I woke around midnight and made broth, which had a slight restorative effect. We started to look forward to living, rather than dying.

In the morning light we began to negotiate the Wrangell Narrows, an important transition: we all had the same remembered past from here south. I could stop watching what I said, in that regard.

There was an interesting surprise waiting for us at

the dock—dozens of prospectors who had changed their plans, going inland along the Stikine River, the route everyone had taken to the Yukon before the Chilkoot Pass had opened. With Skagway closed down for an indefinite period, these men had chosen the somewhat longer alternative.

And they needed more supplies.

A broker came on deck and offered a blanket 10 percent over what we had paid in the States, for anything. Then, we found out, he turned around and sold it piecemeal with a 25 percent markup.

Doc was sure he could bypass the broker and make a quick profit. He went to the boys about splitting the kit to sell his third, and they surprised him by saying "sell it all."

It was a little unfair, I supposed; they were dispirited by the day of violent illness and confused and upset by the developments in Skagway. If I had been an objective parent, I would have counseled them to wait a few days before deciding to give it up. Instead, I pounced on the chance.

From my diary I had a list of everything and its price. I copied it out and added 25 percent, while the men were offloading the kit to the far end of Front Street, which was serving as a kind of trading post. Chuck borrowed some paint and printed on a plank

EVRYTHING GOS, which made me cringe, but did the job.

Doc and I carried two boxes of books out to the school. Grace Logan was ecstatic, and sent her three biggest boys back to carry the rest.

By the time we'd finished that, our own boys had sold more than half of the supplies, and were stunned by the amount of money they suddenly had—$1,400 in bills and coin and gold dust.

Doc went around comparing prices, and found that our inventory was going so fast because other people's markups here were greater than 25 percent. We sent the boys into town for an alcoholic hangover cure and took over the selling, with an additional 10 percent markup. We sold almost everything before sundown, and got back aboard the *White Nights* with $2,591 and a box of cans of sardines.

We ate sardines all the way to Nunaimo, three days, and I've never opened a can of them since.

The view from midcentury.

Doc and I were married by a city official in Seattle. The four of us had a long talk, and we decided not to risk the family fortune on oranges or artichokes, but to move back to the Midwest.

I believe my second son was conceived one night on the Pullman car that took us back to Missouri. I named him Gordon, for reasons I could never tell anyone, and also gave him Doc's Christian name Charles.

Last year, in 1951, Charles Gordon Coleman was awarded the Nobel Prize in physics. He changed the world, this world, I hope for the better.

Other interesting things happened between his birth and his journey to Stockholm.

We bought acreage in Rolla and turned it into a fairly successful farm, with various crops rotating through the seasons—what they call a truck farm now. Chuck is still on the farm today, a white-bearded patriarch. My Daniel had no patience for it, and after a year went off to sea with the merchant marine.

He joined the navy in World War I and perished when his ship was torpedoed by a German submarine.

Strange to write those words. He also died in a gunfight in Dawson City. Both deaths were real, and the first one hurt more than the second.

I taught high school in Rolla for twenty years, part-time, as I was making more money in my second career, writing pulp fiction. I wrote at least one story a week, under a variety of male pseudonyms—westerns, science fiction, mysteries—and the occasional romance, under my own false name, Rosa Coleman.

That figured in one of the strangest meetings of my life. I was shopping in Rolla in the summer of 1905, and sat down on a park bench to rest and cool off. A large man sat down on the other end of the bench.

"Rosa Coleman," he said, and I looked up, expecting one of my readers. There were several such in Rolla. His face seemed vaguely familiar, but he wasn't a local.

He gave me a mysterious smile. "Or is it Rosa Tolliver?"

I stood and fought the impulse to flee. "Who are you?"

"We were never formally introduced. My name is William Sizemore. Late of the Pinkerton agency." Of course. The last time I'd seen him, he was lying on the floor, bleeding, only the whites of his eyes showing.

"I'll . . . I'm glad to see that you're alive."

He rubbed the back of his head. "Was it your son who slugged me?" I nodded. "Pretty good job."

"You've been tracking us for seven years?"

"Hardly." He took off his hat and mopped his forehead. "I caught up with you in Wrangell in ninety-eight on your way back to the States." All I could do was look at him.

"You should never have pawned the revolver. Along the bottom of the barrel, it was stamped 'Property of the Pinkerton Agency,' and had an identification number. I was fired for not having reported it lost—but I was about to quit anyhow.

"I didn't like your husband, the first one, and suspected that *your* story was the true version. I decided to lie—protecting myself as well as you—and telegraphed him that you had disappeared during a bad storm the previous winter, and were missing and presumed dead. It was child's play to steal a missing-persons form from the Dodge City Police Department. Your son was presumably headed for the Philippines.

"I followed your trail to Seattle, and found people who remembered you as the lone woman on the Russian freighter. I was headed for Skagway when the troubles there closed it, and found that the ship was returning.

"I waited in Wrangell, pretty well disguised as a scruffy prospector. Haggled for supplies with your son and his friend, and then followed them to a bar when you and Doc showed up. We talked for awhile and I got your cover story.

"Followed you back to Seattle and saw the marriage announcement. Left you alone then, biding my time in Philadelphia, until now."

"What's happened now?"

"Edward remarried early this year. But it didn't last." He unrolled the newspaper he was holding, a week-old *Philadelphia Inquirer*. There was a front-page story, "MILLIONAIRE LAWYER FOUND DEAD— Police suspect Young Wife in Poisoning."

"She's actually admitted to it," he said. "Even if she doesn't go to jail, she won't get a penny of his fortune. I think it's time for you to reappear."

"As his long-lost wife? I'm not married to him anymore."

"No one in Philadelphia knows that but me. And for ten percent, I'll never tell."

"Ten percent of how much?"

"More than two million dollars."

Of course I considered it, if just for a few moments. I tried to express my feelings to Mr. Sizemore. "Even if the millions came with no strings attached, I would hesitate."

"That's hard to believe."

"I've had millions. It was the most miserable time of my life."

"But you would *really* have them now! You could buy anything for yourself and your family."

"Not without explaining where the money came from."

"A rich relative died."

"And if anyone—like Edward's nasty sister!—was curious and did the slightest investigation, it would come out that I was married to two men, and defrauded Edward's relatives out of the money. I'd lose the money and go to prison."

"I think a good lawyer who knew the true circumstances could prevent both."

"To the shame, and perhaps loss, of my actual family."

He shook his head. "Consider this. The only link to your actual past is me. I would never tell anyone the truth, because my ten percent would look like extortion, then."

What is it now, I thought. But he hadn't threatened to expose me.

He handed me a business card. "This is too much, too fast for you. Think it over. I'll be at the Hotel Central for a week. Please reconsider." He turned to go.

"Mr. Sizemore. You've gone to considerable expense to come out here. Let me reimburse—"

"You have even less money than I," he said with a quaver in his voice that might have been anger. Then he walked out of my life.

I read through the Philadelphia paper and did feel a pang at the announcements and advertisements. The opera, fine restaurants, the new moving pictures and automobiles. I lazily considered a scenario where I would go to Philadelphia and collect the money, and then a few months later, meet a nice widower from Missouri; fall in love with him and marry, and we would live wealthily ever after.

But then Doc and Chuck and even Gordon would have to know the whole story, and live a lie for the rest of their lives.

I thought of mailing the article to Daniel, so he would know that the monster was dead. But no need to open old wounds. I folded up the paper and dropped it in the trash.

. . .

It would be foolish to pretend I have never regretted that decision. There's an old joke about farming: a rich relative dies and leaves a million dollars to a farmer. A newspaperman asks him what he plans to do with all that cash. He scratches his chin and says, "Guess I'll keep farmin' till the money runs out."

The farm sustained us, though, through generations. Chuck married in 1902 and continued the Coleman dynasty. We survived the Depression and, through luck of geography, the Dust Bowl.

I was never much more than an accessory to the farm. I put up vegetables and did the bookkeeping and the research to schedule rotation. But my main contribution was money, and it wasn't tainted money from Edward's family fortune.

The farmhouse we'd bought in the Rolla estate sale came complete with a ten-year-old Remington typewriter that almost worked. Doc fixed it up and I learned how to type by writing dime novels. The first one sold for more than the farm had made in its best month! So at the age of forty-three, I embarked upon a new career.

I had never written a story before, but had committed reams of poetry as a child, and had the required composition courses at Wellesley—plus a million or so words in my diaries. I can't say that anything I wrote approached being literature. But I had great fun, and people paid me for it!

Gordon didn't like farming much more than his older brother had, but he pitched in with a kind of grim determination. Science was his passion. He made his own telescope and turned a spare storeroom into a chemistry lab, which he almost burned down a couple of times.

He had a serious accident the summer before he started high school—his foot caught in a combine and he lost most of the toes. That got him out of a lot of farm work, and also saved him from the war that took his brother.

Gordon was offered a scholarship to Princeton in 1917, and graduated with honors. He went to Harvard for his Ph.D., and returned to Princeton to study and teach. His mentor was the atomic pioneer

Leo Szilard, and they were coequals by the time they both disappeared into the wilds of New Mexico. "War work" was all he could tell me.

Years later, I would find out about the Manhattan Project, and how Gordon had changed the course of history.

The original Project had planned for the production of two devastatingly powerful A-bombs, Fat Man and Little Boy, which would be dropped on Japanese cities and kill millions, mostly women and children and old men. We would end the war with one vicious strike.

Gordon calculated that the precious U-235 could be redistributed so that a third bomb, Baby Boy, could give them a possible weapon for peace. Einstein convinced Truman to okay the strategy, and so Baby Boy was dropped into Tokyo Bay as a demonstration. There was little loss of life, but a dramatic mushroom cloud hovered over the city for a long time. The High Command and Emperor knew about the other two bombs, and knew they would be in the air the next day, and Japan capitulated.

So millions of lives were spared, American as well as Japanese, because if Manhattan had failed, they were going to invade and take Japan inch by terrible inch. Millions of lives allowed to continue, because a half-century ago on another world, Raven walked through my door and I listened to him.

Guardian of life. Because I lived, and gave birth, the World War didn't end in a nuclear holocaust.

It occurs to me now that Raven didn't stop there. Of course he went ahead into myriad futures, nudging humanity away from Armageddon. Why, and in whose service? I never thought to ask; he may well have had a simple answer. That ignorance has haunted me for half a century.

Other than Daniel, I've only told two people about Raven. One was a psychiatrist I went to in 1918, to help me deal with the grief and helplessness I felt, losing my firstborn twice.

He listened with interest for several sessions, and then told me gently that I had built up a remarkably complex and consistent set of delusions in order to deal with intolerable memories: the recent grief and the old one, the sexual violence Edward had delivered to me and our son. He said that at my age, and in my situation, the best thing would be to continue believing the Raven story was true—as long as I didn't tell anybody else about it!—because it amounted to a belief system that allowed me to think that Daniel was still alive, in some millions of alternative universes where the torpedo missed his ship.

I could almost believe him—like most analysts of the time, he had the shrunken heart of a master salesman—because his belief system was as internally consistent as my own, and he had the beard and couch and framed diplomas to reinforce its reality.

It doesn't explain the new dress, though. Fifty-five years ago I greeted my dead son and forced him to admit I was wearing a dress that I hadn't owned a few hours before—in fact, it was the only copy of that dress in the whole world, because it didn't appear in catalogs until the next month. It also didn't explain my instant acquisition of Tlingit language and lore.

The analyst tacitly accepted both as necessary lies. I came to realize that I could stay on that couch until the next ice age, and never dislodge him from his pinnacle of Freudian certainty. So I said good-bye and made him the villain in a novella in *Spicy Detective*.

The only other man I've told was the magazine publisher and editor Hugo Gernsback. On a whim I went to New York in 1930, Christmas shopping for the grandchildren. It was a strange bleak time for most people, little work and low wages even if you found some. But the penny or two per word that I got from Gernsback and his rivals, at as much as two thousand words a day, made us a comparatively wealthy family. So after I stood in the crowd and watched the window displays at Macy's and Gimbel's, I could actually go inside and buy things, armloads, and have them delivered to my hotel. As I'd done at older stores when I was young and rich.

I'd read in the letters column of Gernsback's *Science Wonder Quarterly* about a science fiction club called the Scienceers, who met every week or so in New York City. I'd written down the address, and took a cab there without calling ahead.

They were a bunch of earnest young men, not quite prepared for a seventy-two-year-old woman to show up and claim she was Lance Williams, author of the Zodiac Jones series. But one of their members was David Lasser, the editor of *Science Wonder Stories,* the magazine that ran my series. He called up the publisher, Hugo Gernsback, and the great man actually drove through the snow to meet me.

He was a strange, intense man, of middle years but crackling with energy. He was delighted to find out that I was a woman, and an *old* woman at that.

After a few minutes he declared that the place was too smoky for him, and I emphatically agreed, so he asked me whether I would care to come have a cup of coffee with him.

The city sky was sparkling with winter stars, which

I don't suppose would be possible today. He pointed out the Great Nebula in the sword of Orion, and told me astronomers thought new stars, new worlds, were birthing there.

I took a deep breath and told him that I knew it was true. I'd been there.

He listened to me for an hour or more, walking along and then in the café, quietly asking pointed questions.

I think he half believed me, but then he believed many strange things. He made me a business proposition: write it up as an "as-told-to" interview, Lance Williams talking to an old lady who claimed to have had this experience. He would devote most of an issue of his new "scientifiction" magazine *Amazing* to it, presenting it as fact, and see what the response was. Maybe my Raven had visited other people, and this would make them come forward.

It sounded like a good idea to me. Most readers would accept it as fiction, done with a clever angle, but indeed there might be people out there who could corroborate my story. I did suspect it had happened to four other writers—Flammarion, of course, and also Homer, William Blake, and Jonathan Swift. (Swift left a message in *Gulliver's Travels,* describing the tiny moons of Mars 150 years before Asaph Hall discovered them, coincidentally at the same time that I was studying astronomy in college.)

I couldn't tell the whole story, sodomy and all, in a pulp magazine then—and couldn't now, twenty years later—so I substituted whippings and verbal abuse, as I had when I related the story to Gernsback.

If I'd known he was about to start publishing the magazine *Sexology,* I might have confided in him.

The "interview" took up half of the April 1931 issue of the magazine, and the $580 Gernsback paid for it was most welcome. But the two letters I got from people who claimed to be fellow travelers were evidence of something more ordinary than my experience.

World without end.

I continued writing off and on for the next decade, but paper shortages during the War closed down most of my markets.

By then I was doing more church work than anything else, and enjoying my grandchildren and great-grandchildren.

I suppose I went back to the church to fill the hole in my life left when Doc passed away in 1935. He'd had six more years than his allotted three score and ten, and simple people, I think, were surprised by the intensity of my grief. *You must have known his days were numbered,* they were thinking. My days, too, then as now, and yours no less than mine.

But love's not time's fool, the poet said. In its quiet way, our love was more intense in old age than it had been when we started our new lives together. We did a lot of things then that we couldn't have done when the farm sucked up all his daylight hours and some of the night and morning dark.

After Chuck took over the farm, we went to see Picasso and Miró at a Chicago exhibition in the late twenties, and Doc's view of the world was transformed. I taught him what I could of oil painting, and in the few years he had left, he quite surpassed me with his energetic primitivism. He didn't care to show his paintings; they were to him just a natural and necessary part of life. He could and should have been another late-blooming Whistler. But he valued privacy far above praise, and I loved him for that as much as for anything else.

So when I lost him it was a hammer blow. Of course I expected it, but it was never going to be this year, this week, this day. One day he woke feeling poorly, and asked me to drive him to the doctor, and he died of a heart attack before we got there.

And so I wandered back into the fold. I wasn't religious—my Raven had cured me of believing in simple answers—but old ladies have to do something or they'll dry up and blow away.

I could hardly do missionary work anymore, but I was active in the church's Ladies' Auxiliary, mostly visiting the sick and the old with flowers and sweets, reading to them, commiserating.

Last Sunday was Easter, and the night before, the minister had been rushed to the hospital with appendicitis. An elder called and asked me whether, as the oldest member of the congregation, I would be willing to stand up and give a few words of witness.

My heart was both melancholy and merry as I assured the respectful congregation that I faced death with equanimity, because I was certain that death was not the end—that we all would wind up in a quieter place, free of pain and worry.

I didn't tell them that they'd be sharing the place with sinners, not to mention dinosaurs and huge worms and creatures made of metal or vapors. Nor that it was a gray plane that went on and on to no horizon.

Some of that might have been in my voice, though. A lot of them were visibly relieved when I changed the subject and asked that we all offer a prayer of hope for our men overseas, and God's guidance to General LeMay and his new air force, that they not use the terrible weapons left over from World War II on Korea. Some faces hardened at that. But I didn't want to see Gordon's miracle of peace undone.

Both Gordons, human and otherwise.

I suppose it's time to stop, and let this document drift into the future. Futures. You who read it may choose to consider it fiction, or even delusion.

There is always some truth in both.